She had no right to dream of a relationship with Walker

Or even to want one. She'd imposed on his hospitality and pleaded with him to give her refuge. He'd already gone beyond what most men would have done. To take further advantage of the friendship he'd offered when her own life was still in disarray would be the height of unfairness to them both.

Which didn't mean she couldn't admire his seat in a saddle, the way he moved as though part of his mount, the man and animal of the same mind as they walked beside the herd. A man of the land comfortable with himself.

Yes, she could admire, but she didn't dare touch. Because she was confident, once she touched Walker in an intimate way and he touched her in return, that she'd never be satisfied with anything less....

Dear Reader,

What a special lineup of love stories Harlequin American Romance has for you this month. Bestselling author Cathy Gillen Thacker continues her family saga, THE DEVERAUX LEGACY, with *His Marriage Bonus*. A confirmed bachelor ponders a marital merger with his business rival's daughter, and soon his much-guarded heart is in danger of a romantic takeover!

Next, a young woman attempts to catch the eye of her lifelong crush by undergoing a head-to-toe makeover in *Plain Jane's Plan*, the latest book in Kara Lennox's HOW TO MARRY A HARDISON miniseries. In *Courtship, Montana Style* by Charlotte Maclay, a sophisticated city slicker arrives on a handsome rancher's doorstep, seeking refuge with a baby in her arms. *The Rancher Wore Suits* by Rita Herron is the first book in TRADING PLACES, an exciting duo about identical twin brothers separated at birth who are reunited and decide to switch places to see what their lives might have been like.

Enjoy this month's offerings, and be sure to return each and every month to Harlequin American Romance!

Happy reading,

Melissa Jeglinski
Associate Senior Editor
Harlequin American Romance

COURTSHIP, MONTANA STYLE
Charlotte Maclay

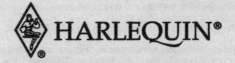

TORONTO • NEW YORK • LONDON
AMSTERDAM • PARIS • SYDNEY • HAMBURG
STOCKHOLM • ATHENS • TOKYO • MILAN • MADRID
PRAGUE • WARSAW • BUDAPEST • AUCKLAND

Special thanks to Joan Sweeney, who willingly shared both good and bad memories of growing up in Montana. Yours is a life worth celebrating. Cherish every moment as I cherish our friendship.

ISBN 0-373-16943-4

COURTSHIP, MONTANA STYLE

Copyright © 2002 by Charlotte Lobb.

Visit us at www.eHarlequin.com

Printed in U.S.A.

ABOUT THE AUTHOR

Charlotte Maclay can't resist a happy ending. That's why she's had such fun writing more than twenty titles for Harlequin American Romance, Duets and Love & Laughter, plus several Silhouette Romance books, as well. Charlotte is particularly well-known for her volunteer efforts in her hometown of Torrance, California; her philosophy is that you should make a difference in your community. She and her husband have two married daughters and four grandchildren, whom they are occasionally allowed to baby-sit. She loves to hear from readers and can be reached at P.O. Box 505, Torrance, CA 90508.

Books by Charlotte Maclay

HARLEQUIN AMERICAN ROMANCE

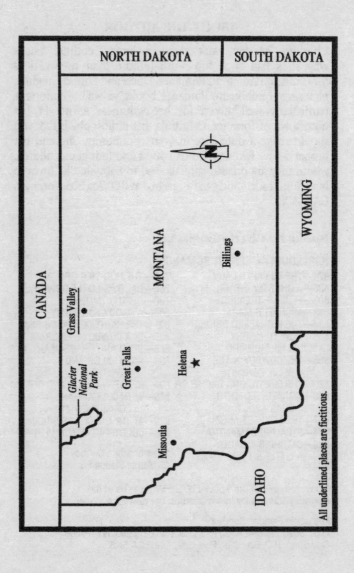

NORTH DAKOTA

SOUTH DAKOTA

CANADA

WYOMING

MONTANA

Billings

Grass Valley

Glacier National Park

Great Falls

Helena

Missoula

IDAHO

All underlined places are fictitious.

Chapter One

"There is no question, my dear, you will be the most beautiful bride Marin County has ever seen. *Trés elegant.* Your wedding will be *the* social occasion of the year."

The owner of Gloriana's Bridal Boutique hovered around Elizabeth Tilden, all part of the service in the most extravagant bridal shop in the most exclusive county in California, located across the bay from San Francisco.

Gloriana lifted the veil from Elizabeth's head and clipped it to a hanger. "I know you will not be as foolish as one of our patrons, a young lady who walked out of the church at the very last minute last week with the groom already standing at the altar. Such a waste. All that food at the reception and such a lovely gown." The boutique owner made a tsking sound and shook her head.

Elizabeth wondered if canceling the wedding meant the woman was foolish—or *courageous,* a trait Elizabeth sorely lacked. She hated disappointing anyone and shied away from confrontation. For as long as she could remember, she'd been a *nice* girl.

But sometimes *nice* girls finished last.

Where had that other bride found the backbone to walk away from her own wedding?

Lowering the zipper at the back of Elizabeth's gown, Gloriana said, "I have no such fears you will do such a naughty thing, walking out on your handsome husband-to-be. Your family would be so upset. Yours is one wedding day that will go off like clockwork, as they say."

With care, Elizabeth stepped out of the tulle-and-lace gown with its rows and rows of tiny pearls and grand sweeping train. She felt far less confident about her fast-approaching wedding day than Gloriana did.

Three days to go, and what Elizabeth saw in the full-length mirror was a reluctant bride. Not terrified. Not simply getting cold feet or having second thoughts. But a bride who no longer believed marriage to Vernon Sprague was the smart thing to do, no matter how vigorously her family encouraged her match to the wealthy investment counselor.

But she'd never have the audacity to risk a terrible scene with her mother. Or Vernon, for that matter. Hadn't she already buckled under their combined wishes more times than she cared to count? If only things had turned out differently....

She'd grown up a member of the country-club set and met Steve Poling when she was an awkward twelve-year-old. For her it had been love at first sight. Or perhaps adoration was a better word.

It took Steve several years to notice her, but by high school they started dating. At least while she was home for summer vacations they saw each other. He was fun to be with, bringing an excitement into her otherwise restricted life. His bold even sometimes reckless behavior appealed to her.

By the time Elizabeth entered college, they were dating each other exclusively—except she attended a private women's college in New England and he was studying petroleum engineering at UCLA. After they both graduated they planned to marry. But first Steve wanted to get his career on solid footing. Then came his chance for a grand adventure—an oil exploration trip to the Amazon River basin. He couldn't resist the opportunity.

Only after he'd left town had she realized she was pregnant. Steve hadn't hesitated once he learned she was expecting. He arranged to fly home. They'd marry—

Even after a year, Elizabeth's throat still tightened on the painful knowledge that if he hadn't been coming home to marry her in haste his plane never would have crashed. He'd be alive today. And they'd be together, she, the man she'd loved all through adolescence and the baby they'd created together.

A small army of assistants dressed as French maids flitted into the private dressing room, scooping up the gown and veil to be safely wrapped for the trip to Elizabeth's home and thence to the same church on Saturday that had seen equally extravagant weddings for three prior generations of Morley-Tilden women.

Still in her satin slip, Elizabeth sat down after everyone had left the dressing room. Despite her worries, she smiled at the precious sleeping baby in the carrier she'd placed on the floor next to the plush-velvet couch. *Suzanne.*

Her baby...and Steven's.

As unintended as her pregnancy had been, Suzanne was now her life. Her love.

That was far from the case for Vernon, who had shown little interest in her three-month-old daughter.

Elizabeth's parents had been heartsick—and embarrassed—to learn she was pregnant and unwed, a social scandal, they'd said. With grief weighing her down, Elizabeth had agreed to become engaged to Vernon Sprague, a wealthy investment counselor with considerable political clout. The perfect brother-in-law to enhance her brother Robert's political ambitions. The marriage—of money, influence and wealth—would take place after the baby's birth. There would be no disgrace for the Tilden name.

Through a haze of despair and guilt, Elizabeth had agreed to the arrangement. As usual she had given in to the wishes of her prominent family.

But now she was responsible for another person's future happiness. She needed to decide what was best not only for herself but for her baby as well, a far more important decision.

She ran her fingertips over the blond fuzz on the top of Suzanne's head, so light in color it was barely visible and as soft as down. A deep, abiding love filled Elizabeth's chest, making it difficult to draw a breath.

How in heaven's name could she raise her daughter to be a strong woman when she'd always been such a weakling?

Since her morning visit with her older sister, Elizabeth had more doubts than ever about her impending marriage. Victoria, like their mother, lived with the knowledge of her husband's infidelities and was miserable because of it.

Not only had this past year left Elizabeth with nagging questions about Vernon's faithfulness, but he'd already talked about hiring a nanny and sending Suzanne to boarding school as soon as she was old enough.

Elizabeth balked at the suggestion and they'd had a terrible argument, the issue as yet unresolved. But she vowed she would *never* give her baby over for someone else to raise. She'd experienced too much of that in her own childhood.

Struggling with indecision, idly she picked up a women's magazine on the coffee table and flipped through the pages. An article caught her eye about Montana's Foster Dad of the Year, a rancher in a remote part of the state who provided refuge for unwanted children.

That's what Elizabeth and her baby needed. *A refuge.* A place where she would have the time and freedom to decide what was best for their future without the interference of her family and the pressure she had so much trouble resisting.

She was such a *wimp* when it came to wanting to please her family.

That's why simply moving into an apartment of her own wouldn't do, although she could easily afford to live on her own because of the trust fund her grandmother had left her. She needed to be far away from her family. And Vernon. In an entirely different state where she'd avoid any chance they'd find her, confront her, and she'd bow to their will once again.

In her heart, she knew starting a new life was the best thing she could do for her daughter.

Reading down the page, her gaze landed on a quote in bold type from Walker Oakes, the rancher in question. *"We're pretty self-sufficient here on the ranch, but with this many teenage boys it would sure be nice to have a housekeeper."*

A *housekeeper.*

That wasn't such a hard job. Not that Elizabeth had any experience to qualify her for that kind of employment. But how difficult could it be to dust and vacuum and put a load of wash on? Surely a college graduate who spoke Italian, German and French with some fluency could handle the job with a minimum of effort.

With a mental stiffening of her spine, she glanced one more time at the article, folded the magazine and tucked it beside Suzanne in the car seat. That's where she and her baby would go, to Montana, as unlikely a place as she could imagine. No one in her world would come looking for her there, certainly not on a remote ranch where she'd be an anonymous housekeeper.

If that other bride had found the courage to walk out on her wedding day, Elizabeth could drum up

enough spunk to leave now before it was too late—
and escape the confrontations she so dreaded.

For Suzanne's sake, she could do it because she
couldn't imagine raising her child in a household
where her father ignored her.

As her own father had been indifferent to her.

The only remaining problem was to avoid leaving
a trail that would lead Vernon or her family to her
secret hideaway in Montana before she reached her
decisions. To make her admittedly impetuous scheme
work, she'd have to be resourceful—and lucky.

She'd also have to lie convincingly, another talent
she lacked. For the sake of Suzanne's future, she'd
damn well learn! This was no time to let her well-
developed conscience get the upper hand.

This cowboy's ranch was going to be a refuge for
both her and her baby. Meanwhile, she'd pretend to
be someone she wasn't—a strong, determined woman
who could handle a dust mop as well as the next
woman. If her acting was good enough, maybe she'd
actually become that confident person.

A half hour later, with her wedding gown in the
trunk of her BMW and Suzanne still dozing comfortably in her car seat, Elizabeth drove to her bank to
make a substantial withdrawal. Later she'd call her
mother to assure her that she was safe—and ask her
to cancel the wedding. Speaking to her on the phone
would be much easier than in person.

Worst case, she could hang up and turn off her cell
phone.

STEPPING UP ONTO THE BACK porch of his ranch house,
Walker Oakes slapped his Stetson against his thigh

and stomped his boots. Dust billowed up like a miniature tornado.

By June the rangeland in this part of northern Montana should have been boot deep with nutritious grass for his cattle to graze. Instead a cold, dry winter had led into an even dryer spring, stunting the grass, leaving barely enough for the prairie dogs to nibble on. The lightest breeze stirred up a dust devil. Riding herd on his cattle meant eating dirt from dawn to dusk.

Muttering a curse under his breath, he went into the house and hooked his hat on a peg in the mudroom.

The well-equipped kitchen was huge with a table big enough to seat a dozen people when stretched to its limit. This time of year it only had to handle five: himself, the three boys currently in his foster care and Speed Pendrix, his foreman, the slowest talking, slowest moving man north or south of the Missouri River. A man Walker Oakes would trust with his life, and had more than once.

Walker needed to know the going price for beef cattle so he headed for his office to check online. Unless they got rain and got it damn soon, he was going to have to cull his herd, getting rid of cows that hadn't produced a calf this spring. He might even have to sell off some of the yearlings at half the price he'd be able to get after a summer's grazing fattened them up. Sometimes to save a ranch a man had to walk a tightrope, making tough decisions.

As he walked through the living room with its big

rock fireplace and heavy, overstuffed furniture, he heard a car approaching the ranch house. He glanced outside as it stopped in front.

Most of his Grass Valley neighbors came to visit via the back door. None that he could think of drove a fancy silver-blue BMW that looked near new. Like him, pickups were more their style.

Curious, he opened the door, shoved open the screen and stepped outside into the warmth of late afternoon.

The young woman who exited the BMW was a sweet little filly with flaxen hair she had pulled into some kind of a twist at the back of her head. So slender a good wind would blow her over, he wondered if, like his cows, she wasn't getting enough feed lately. Still, she moved with the grace of a dancer and was a mighty pretty sight after riding herd all day on cows and all night on adolescent boys filled with a combination of rebellion and hormones they didn't know how to tame. And the way she filled out a pair of city slicker blue jeans was something to write home about.

He stepped off the porch at the same time Bandit, a black-and-white mostly Border collie rounded the corner and took up a position beside him, tail wagging watchfully.

"Can I help you, miss?" Walker asked. No doubt he'd have to direct her where she had intended to be, which surely wasn't at the Double O Ranch.

Standing in full sunlight, the stranger shaded her eyes with her hand. "I'm looking for Walker Oakes."

That was a surprise. She wasn't lost after all, though

she didn't look like she belonged anywhere more Western than a dude ranch. "You found him."

"Oh, good. I'm, uh, Lizzie Thomas. I'm here about the job."

Job? He hired extra hands during roundup and hayharvest time, but none that looked like this woman.

He walked toward the stranger so he wouldn't have to yell—and so he could get a better look at her. Dutifully Bandit remained at his heel.

As he drew closer, Walker decided his visitor was worth more than a second look. She had the face of a Greek goddess with high cheekbones, slightly pouty lips and a complexion no rancher's wife could ever achieve, however many gallons of skin cream she applied.

"Sorry. You must have the wrong place. I'm not hiring right now." Not extra cowhands or a woman with pure, unadulterated sex appeal.

"Unless you've already filled the position..." Turning, she opened the BMW's back door. A moment later, she produced a baby's car seat—

Walker's eyes widened.

—with the baby included.

"I'd like to apply to be your housekeeper."

"Housekeep—?" He choked, feeling as off balance as though someone had slipped him a rogue bronc when he wasn't looking. "Is this some kind of a joke?"

Bandit crept forward, sat down and cocked his head. His tail continued to slowly sweep the ground as he craned for a better look at the baby.

Casting a quick smile in the dog's direction, the woman hooked her arm through the car seat handle, holding it in front of her. With her free hand, she handed him a magazine. "According to this article, you need a housekeeper. I'm applying."

He shook his head. "You've got a baby," he said stupidly. "You can't possibly expect—"

"I didn't think in government service you were allowed to discriminate."

He frowned. This Lizzie person had the most intense blue eyes, which were currently zapping him with blue-lightning strikes. "I'm not a government employee," he pointed out, and suddenly he'd lost all interest in Western hospitality. Which wasn't like him at all. He was an easygoing guy. Friendly with everybody. Which meant maybe the boys had figured out how to play a practical joke on him, and he should just go along.

"Perhaps not, but you do take money from the government to assist in the support of the foster children placed in your care."

A muscle twitched in his jaw. None of this sounded right, and it sure as hell wasn't funny. Was she accusing him of stealing the money? "I spend every dime of that money on the kids."

"Of course. Nonetheless, accepting government funds means you cannot discriminate against working mothers. It's the law."

What the hell! He'd never discriminated against anyone. Ever! He liked women. Even mothers. A lot! And now this sexy female was telling him—

"Hey, boss, what's goin' on?" Speed Pendrix sauntered around the corner of the house, his loose-limbed walk somewhere between a stroll and a full stop.

Moving at the same pace, Bandit got up to greet the foreman.

"This woman says I've got to hire her to be my housekeeper," Walker told Speed.

"Well, now, ain't that nice." He ambled up to the car, a big, foolish grin on his face as he took in Lizzie and the baby, who was dressed in pink overalls and a matching denim cap. "Don't ya know, we surely could use some housekeeping help and darned if she's not the purdiest little thing I've seen in a month of Sundays."

"Why, thank you, Mr...."

"Jest call me Speed, ma'am. Everybody does." He tipped his wide-brimmed straw hat.

Extending her hand, Lizzie granted the foreman a radiant smile that would have curled Walker's toes if it had been meant for him. Which it wasn't. All she'd done was shoot daggers in his direction. And he'd shot them back, he admitted. But he'd had reason, damn it!

"It's nice to meet you, Speed."

"Cain't say as I remember a time when we had a baby around here. It'll be a nice change."

"Now wait a minute," Walker objected. "She can't come waltzing in here and expect—"

His three-man crew of adolescents came bursting out of the house, the screen door banging against its stop. They leaped off the steps—Bean Pole stumbling as he landed—and surrounded the woman and her car. Bandit wove his way between the adolescents' legs.

"Yo, man! Look at them wheels!"

"Hey, she's got a baby. My mom had a baby."

"Bet I could get you fifty, maybe sixty bucks for those cool hubcaps. You wanna sell, lady?"

"Hold it!" Walker bellowed. He'd lost control of the situation and he damn well was going to get it back.

The boys snapped to attention. Even the woman pulled her shoulders back, her expression startled and wide-eyed.

"Let's take this whole thing a little slower," Walker said. "This lady is—"

"Lizzie Thomas," she repeated.

"From?" he prodded.

"Merry Maids, Inc."

Which Walker had never heard of but, based on the out-of-state license plates on her car, he concluded it was in Nevada. "And you're here because?"

"Because you stated very clearly in this magazine article that you need a housekeeper."

She spoke in a reasonable tone, her voice slightly bluesy and very sexy, yet it wasn't a reasonable statement at all. He didn't need a housekeeper. Well, he did, but he couldn't afford one and he sure as hell wasn't equipped to house a woman *and* her baby at the ranch.

"Wow! That's great!" Scotty, the youngest of the boys at age twelve, leaned forward to chuck the baby under her chin.

"Your hands are dirty, son," Walker warned.

"No, they're not. I washed 'em—"

"Enough! I'm not going to start an argument about dirty hands. We're going to start from the beginning and do this right." So Walker could get to the bottom of what was going on.

"These are my foster sons, Miss Thomas. Take off your hats, boys." They all responded, even Speed. "Scotty here is the one enamored of the baby. His real name is Donald MacLeod and you can figure his red hair is one of the reasons we call him Scotty."

"Hello, Scotty. It's fine if you want to touch Suzanne. A little dirt won't hurt her."

Walker scowled. This was *his* show, *his* ranch. No pretty little filly with a quick smile and long, red fingernails was going to muscle her way in here without his say-so. Which he wasn't about to give.

"Our resident expert on the value of assorted car parts is Fridge—Arnold Bullock," Walker continued. "He can empty a refrigerator in one sitting and a junkyard in about fifteen minutes, if you give him a chance. Which we try not to do."

Her amused smile shot a flush to the boy's cheeks, which were just beginning to show the first signs of growing whiskers.

"And Bean Pole here is Chad Stringer, one of my best cowhands on a horse." On land, he was so clumsy he was barely able to walk around without falling over his own feet, a trait Walker recalled all too clearly from his own adolescent years. "He outgrows a pair of jeans faster than Fridge can empty the refrigerator.''

Lizzie nodded to the boys. "I'm glad to meet all of you."

"You've met Speed, my foreman, and the dog's name is Bandit."

She smiled at the dog and reached down to let Bandit smell the back of her hand. While she petted the top of his head, she kept the baby safely out of the dog's reach.

"Now then, the formalities are taken care of..." He tucked his fingers in his jeans pockets. "I don't know what made you think my comment in that magazine meant I was ready to hire the first housekeeper who showed up at my door. Or *any* housekeeper, for that matter, and certainly not one with a baby. You'll have to go back to wherever—"

"Aw, boss," Scotty complained. "I know how to take care of a baby. I can even change diapers. It's a snap."

Lizzie Thomas seemed unperturbed by Walker's announcement. "Merry Maids anticipated you might need some convincing so they've agreed to cover my salary during my probationary period in order that I might prove my worth to you. So if someone could show me to my quarters?"

She was going to stay? Good God, things were going from bad to worse. And why did she avoid looking him in the eye, her gaze darting away every few seconds like a truant caught out of school? Something was definitely not right here.

"Well, now," Speed drawled, "I'd say that's mighty generous of your employer."

"Can I carry the baby?" Scotty asked. "I'll be real careful."

"Of course." The youngster received another one of her smiles.

"Have you got suitcases and stuff?" Fridge asked. "I can carry them—"

"Wait!" Walker bellowed again. "I guess I didn't make myself clear. We don't need a housekeeper or a baby—"

The baby in question added her own objection, startled awake by Walker's shouting. Speed, all three boys and Miss Thomas hastened to soothe the infant, losing interest in what Walker had to say. In contrast, Bandit retreated to the side of the house, running at a crouch.

Scotty picked the baby up out of the car seat, holding her to his shoulder and patting her on the back with considerable expertise. Meanwhile Lizzie began directing her remaining devotees to her luggage in the BMW's trunk and the baby's supplies in the back seat.

Walker stood in the driveway with about as much animation as a tree stump, having no idea how things had gotten so far out of hand. In a matter of minutes, Lizzie Thomas had bewitched his foreman and his boys. And if the truth were known, she'd come close to doing the same to Walker. That slow, sexy smile of hers and her bluesy voice were enough to make any man rethink the merits of extended celibacy.

Except her story didn't make any sense. Housekeepers didn't simply show up at a man's front door willing to work for nothing. Not when he had adolescent boys in the house who were allergic to baths and cleaning up after themselves.

Nope. Something was screwy about Lizzie Thomas's story. It would be downright interesting to know why she, or someone else, had gone to so much trouble to set up this cockamamy scheme.

For the moment, Walker figured he didn't have much choice but to follow everyone else into the house. Soon enough he'd discover what Lizzie was up to.

And then she'd be gone in a hurry.

As he pulled open the screen door, he caught the lingering scent of a sultry perfume, feminine and inviting, and a little bit tropical. Not the boys. And sure as hell not Speed.

At some gut level, Walker sensed that if Lizzie stuck around very long, the Double O would never be the same.

For the life of him, he couldn't be sure whether that was a good thing—or a bad one.

ELIZABETH STIFLED A SIGH of relief as she entered the house. Never in her life had she been so brazen. *Lied* so blatantly. Or been so rude. But she had managed to get past the first obstacle, which had turned out to be Walker Oakes himself.

The magazine article had been deceiving. From the photo of Walker wearing a Stetson pulled down low on his forehead and a weather-aged sheepskin jacket, she had assumed he'd be a much older man. Not mid-

thirties with saddle-brown hair, an arresting face that
squint lines had filled with character and a rugged physique snugged into skintight jeans. She might well
have given up her plan if she'd known what a formidable opponent he'd be. Nothing like the men in her
life who wore dark suits and ties to work and designer
polo shirts on the golf course.

"Ms. Lizzie, where do you want me to put your
stuff?" Fridge asked.

She shuddered at the nickname she'd given herself.
Her mother would have a fit if she knew, much pre-
ferring the formal version.

"Perhaps we should ask Mr. Oakes his preference?" She tipped her head back to look up at him
with the sweetest expression she could manage. Given
his height, a woman dancing with him would find his
shoulder a perfect spot to rest her head—and she wondered wherever that thought had come from.

Skeptical bronze eyes snared her. "I think you
know my preference."

"Yes, well…" She swallowed hard. He was not
going to be an easy man to fool. "I suppose I could
drive back into town—"

"Now don't you go troubling yourself about driving
anywhere," Speed said. "This here house has got
more bedrooms than you can shake a stick at."

"She could stay in the bunkhouse with us," Bean
Pole volunteered.

Instantly rejecting the idea, Walker told the boy,
"Not on your life."

Ignoring the exchange, Speed continued. "Seems to

me the big 'un across from the boss's would do you just fine. And this here wee little tike—'' he stuck his finger out for the baby to grab ''—she'd be fine in the old sewing room Mrs. Oakes used.''

Elizabeth shot Walker a look. ''Mrs. Oakes?''

''My father's wife. She's been gone from the ranch a long time.''

''Oh.'' A tiny surge of relief skipped through her awareness. The article hadn't, after all, said anything about Walker being married. But it could have been an oversight. And a woman would have seen through her scheme immediately. She'd have recognized Elizabeth didn't know thing one about being a housekeeper.

''I'm sure the sewing room will be perfect for Suzanne,'' she said.

''I'll jest go on upstairs, see to it the room ain't too much of a mess.'' The antithesis of his name, Speed strolled toward the stairway at a pace that would get him to the second floor along about next Tuesday.

''Wait. We haven't got a crib or anything for the baby to sleep in,'' Walker protested.

''That's not a problem,'' Elizabeth assured him. ''I brought a portable playpen along. It's still in the car.'' One of several purchases she'd made in Reno with the cash she'd withdrawn from the bank. She'd then made a side trip to a junkyard where she'd switched license plates with a Jeep that had been totaled, a little trick she'd learned from reading mysteries. With luck, no one would even notice or be able to trace her.

''I'll get the playpen,'' Scotty volunteered.

"No, I will," Fridge insisted. He dropped the suit-case he'd carried in only minutes ago.

"Hold the baby a sec, boss." The boy thrust Suz-anne into Walker's hands. "Fridge doesn't know squat how to put a playpen together. He'll probably bust it."

Both boys went running out the door to the car, Bean Pole traipsing along at a slower pace, leaving Walker standing there, the baby in his big hands, and looking as though Scotty had handed him a bomb that was about to go off.

"Well, hello there, Miss Susie-Q," he said, eyeing the baby with apprehension.

"Here, I'll take her," Elizabeth said.

"Yeah, it might be better if you—"

Suzanne gurgled a happy sound and smiled up at Walker. And then, still smiling, she launched milky spit up all over the front of his blue denim shirt.

Elizabeth groaned and reached for her daughter. She'd really have to teach Suzanne more socially ac-ceptable ways to impress a man.

Chapter Two

Looking down at his shirtfront, Walker winced. "I trust I shouldn't take Susie-Q's comments personally."

"I'm really sorry, Mr. Oakes." Lizzie offered him a cloth diaper in exchange for the baby. "I'm afraid she's having some trouble digesting the formula."

"You might want to consider changing brands."

"I'm sure she'll adjust soon."

Not soon enough for the sake of his shirt, Walker thought as he wiped away the spit up. Despite the mess, he noticed the kid's smile carried a wallop. Just before she hurled her lunch on him, he'd had the fleeting thought that having a baby around the house wouldn't be all that bad. Having a good-looking housekeeper around wouldn't be awful, either.

Susie-Q's milky projectile had brought him back to reality. He hadn't advertised for a housekeeper. Hiring one who had a baby to care for didn't make any sense, even if it didn't cost him a dime. Given that the would-be housekeeper was the sexiest woman he'd seen in a long while would only complicate matters further.

With the boys outside arguing about who would put up the playpen and Speed upstairs doing whatever he was doing, Walker found himself alone with Lizzie. Not a good situation when she was fussing with the baby, looking maternal and feminine. The sounds she made and the gentle way she rocked Susie-Q made him think of lullabies and loving mothers. Not that he'd had much experience with any maternal females except his heifers and their calves.

His own mother hadn't thought enough of Walker to keep him around after she found a new husband.

"Miss Thomas—"

"Why don't you call me Lizzie? It would be so much easier, don't you think?"

No matter what name he called her, it wasn't going to be easy to throw her out, not when his boys were already stuck on her.

"It seems to me—" he began.

"I'm sorry. Is there somewhere I could change Suzanne? She's soaked through."

Now *that* was a really good reason to be nervous about having a baby around the house. They did stuff he didn't know anything about—and didn't want to.

He shrugged helplessly. "Sure. Wherever you want."

Holding the baby on her shoulder, she glanced around the room for a spot that suited her. By now she had a streak of milky stain on her cotton blouse, which had been neatly tucked in at her waist and had tugged free. Her hair was beginning to come loose from its twist. Still there was something glamorous about her, a dose of sophistication Walker wasn't used to. A certain grace that couldn't be learned mucking out stalls.

Walker would lay down a sizable bet in any Nevada gambling casino Lizzie Thomas could name that she was not a housekeeper by trade.

But who the hell was she?

With a flick of her free hand, she tugged a light blanket from the diaper bag the boys had left in the living room and spread it out on the rug. With the ease of a dancer, she settled next to it and lay the baby down.

"There you are, sweetie," she crooned. "I know those old wet diapers are yucky so we'll get you some nice dry ones. How would you like that, huh?"

Susie-Q pumped her chubby little legs, gurgled and blew out a bubble.

In spite of himself, Walker felt his lips tilt into a smile. "Speed's right. She is cute."

As Lizzie lifted her head to bestow one of her smiles on Walker, he felt a punch in the gut that erased everything else in the room except this woman and her baby. He had the eerie sensation she *belonged* there.

But that wasn't possible.

Oliver Oakes had drilled into his head to keep away from fancy women and city slickers. They couldn't make it on a Montana ranch. The winters were too tough; they found the isolation oppressive. They didn't have what it took to be a rancher's wife. Oliver knew.

He'd married one. Within five years he'd lost her and the sons she'd borne him.

In all the years he'd lived with Oliver—since he'd arrived at the Double O as a rebellious fourteen-year-old foster kid—Walker had found the foster father who had eventually adopted him was dead right about most everything he said.

Blinking and shaking his head, Walker knew whatever he'd imagined as he looked down at Lizzie had been caused by months of celibacy and the same isolation that drove women away.

He really needed to get into town more often.

Squatting down on his haunches next to her, he said, "You want to tell me what's going on here?"

"I'm changing Suzanne's diaper."

"I know what you're doing with Susie-Q, what I want to know is—"

"Do you give everyone a nickname?"

He frowned. "I suppose."

"What's yours?"

She was the most distracting woman. Or at least her perfume was. Nothing like the scents he smelled all day, barn smells and prairie sage. Better than both. A scent he could go on inhaling every day and still look forward to taking his first breath the next morning.

He swallowed hard. "Speed and the boys call me boss."

"The boys don't call you Dad?"

"Most of the youngsters who come here have issues about their fathers. No sense to push their buttons. And giving them a nickname gives them a chance to be someone else, someone whose old man hasn't beaten the tar out of them or whose mother didn't abandon him. Someone who can start over without any strikes against them.''

She bent over the baby again, snapping her overalls back together. When she lifted her head, Walker could have sworn there were tears in her eyes, but maybe it was just the light that made the blue glisten like a high-mountain lake on a bright summer day.

''I think that's a wonderful concept,'' she said, her voice huskier than usual. ''And so does Susie-Q, don't you, sweetie?''

She hugged the baby, and something in her eyes brought a lump to Walker's throat. He'd seen that same haunted look in the eyes of the boys who'd come to him over the years. Wary desperation. A need for sanctuary. Fear that he'd turn them out just as their families had.

He didn't doubt for a minute that same look had been in his eyes the day he showed up at the Double O.

Damn it all! How could he send this woman and the baby away? Whatever her real story was, he didn't have the heart to do that.

Not as long as she didn't pose a threat to the Double O Ranch.

''Come on, Slick.'' Standing, he picked up the diaper bag. ''I'll show you to your room.''

Her nicely arched brows rose. ''Slick?''

''Yeah. As in city slicker.''

''What makes you so sure I'm a city slicker?''

"Must be something about that BMW you're driving and the fancy designer label on your rear end." Not to mention her sexy perfume or how nicely her rear end fit into those blue jeans.

As she started to stand, holding the baby to her shoulder with both hands, he took her arm to help her up. His fingers closed around smooth skin, pampered by expensive creams, and warm to the touch. In contrast, his hands were calloused and rough enough to abrade her tender skin.

Pulling his hand away, he tried not to let the velvety feel of her flesh imprint itself into his memory. That was as hopeless as trying to erase a brand from the rump of a calf. No matter how long the animal lived, the evidence of the mark would still be there.

Elizabeth grasped Suzanne more tightly as an unnerving surge of feminine awareness shot through her. During the few seconds Walker touched and then released her, her body had responded in an elemental way to his sheer masculinity, the rugged texture of his palm against her skin in what was little more than a quick caress. Even after he'd let her go, her heartbeat kept up its rapid cadence.

Oddly she'd never reacted in quite that way to a man—not even Steve, whom she had loved with all of her heart, she thought with a stab of guilt. Certainly Vernon hadn't caused her pulse to speed up by simply touching her. She wasn't one to swoon or be dazzled by a handsome face.

Indeed Walker's features were too solid, too sharply honed, to make him a candidate for a *GQ* cover model.

He set his jaw too sharply, pale squint lines fanned out from golden-brown eyes set deeply in his tanned face, and a slight bend in his nose suggested it had once been broken.

No, not a beautiful face but one that was altogether too potently masculine for her taste. Or so she'd thought until he touched her.

"Do you, uh, want me to carry the baby?" he asked, as he walked beside her toward the wide staircase to the second floor. The dark walnut banister looked smoothed by age and, if she knew anything about boys, a thousand youthful slides down it.

"I think for the sake of your shirt, I'd better keep her."

His lips slid into a wry smile. "My shirt's already a loss."

That wasn't quite true. From her perspective, a man with a little baby dribble down his shirt held a certain appeal. It meant he wasn't afraid to be gentle.

Of course, Susie-Q had done more than just dribble. Spitting up hadn't been much of a problem when she was nursing, the baby digesting breast milk far better than she did formula. Not for the first time, she regretted Vernon's demand that she wean Suzanne before the wedding—and her foolish agreement.

She should have stood up for the best interests of her baby. From now on, that's exactly what she was going to do. She'd learn to be strong for Suzanne's sake.

A half-dozen doors led off the upstairs hallway and the carpet was worn thin leading to each room.

"The boys sleep in the bunkhouse?" she asked.

"During the summer. They think of it as one long sleepover. Winter time it's too cold out there and I make 'em sleep inside. Besides, they've gotta get up early to catch the school bus."

"How far is it to their school?"

"About an hour, maybe more, assuming the bus can get through."

"Get through?"

"We get a little snow here now and then."

Elizabeth suspected that was a serious understatement. This close to the Canadian border, winter blizzards had to be as common as wildfires in California.

He gestured toward an open door at the front of the house, and she stepped into the room where Speed was fluffing up a pillow. A light breeze fluttered lace curtains at the windows and brought with it the warm, dry scent of sage.

"Here you go, ma'am." Speed propped the big pillow at the head of the bed. "I gotcha some clean sheets. The blanket might smell a bit musty—"

"This is awfully nice for servants' quarters. Don't you have—"

"Unless you want to bunk with the boys," Walker said, "this is what you get."

Somehow as housekeeper she'd pictured a private room off the kitchen where she and Suzanne would stay, not a guest bedroom opposite her employer's room. She shrugged. "In that case, I'm sure everything will be fine."

The room really was lovely, the view a hundred and

eighty degrees of prairie and rolling, tree-covered hills. In an unpretentious way, the room and view were both more elegant than her parents' home where her mother had spared no expense on furnishings.

Smiling, she imagined Steve would have liked it here. An adventure, he would have said.

A sharp blade of regret slid through her that this adventure was one she and her baby would have to experience without him. Almost a year had passed since she'd laid her beloved Steve to rest and she still felt the raw edge of grief whenever she thought of him. Somehow—for her baby—she had to find a way to go on.

"Miss?"

Blinking back her tears, she turned to the foreman. "Yes?"

"I'll get the boys to bring up your suitcases," Speed said.

Right on cue, the sound of booted feet came thundering down the hallway. Fridge arrived first with the playpen in hand. "Ya want this in here?" he asked Speed.

Complaining at the top of his voice, Scotty arrived lugging Elizabeth's much heavier suitcase, which he'd hauled up from downstairs. "Just 'cuz you're the biggest doesn't mean you're the boss of everybody else!" He dropped the bag by the bed with a thud.

"Put the playpen next door," Walker ordered.

Speed tried to take the folded playpen from Fridge but it popped open, one of the corners catching Speed in the chest and driving him backward.

Bean Pole ambled in with the smaller bag of Suzanne's things and stumbled over the bigger suitcase, barely catching himself before he fell flat on the freshly made bed.

Walker snared the back of the boy's shirt, steadying the youngster as if he'd anticipated a pratfall.

In spite of herself, Elizabeth stifled a grin, not because of the boy's awkwardness but rather the dynamics of the entire Laurel-and-Hardy scene. That Walker was taking the whole situation so calmly spoke volumes about his patience and how well he related to adolescent boys.

Finally wrestling the playpen under control, Speed carried it to a sunny room adjacent to the bedroom.

"I know how to set it up," Fridge insisted, following him.

Scotty dashed in after them. "Don't, either! I had to show you!"

Bean Pole followed. "I can help."

Elizabeth glanced at Walker and he met her gaze, an amused twinkle in his eyes.

"The boys seem very helpful," she commented.

"Normally they avoid every chore I give them until I threaten them with mayhem or no TV for a week. The no TV part works the best."

She imagined so. Despite Walker's rugged appearance, she didn't think his physical threats would be credible. Beneath his rough exterior, he had a gentle spirit. That's what she had sensed in the article and why she'd sought refuge here.

"I'll get the boys out of your hair so you can get

settled. It's about time they started fixing supper anyway.''

"I imagine cooking will be part of my job duties?" she asked with more than a little trepidation. No matter what, she was determined to not sit back and let others wait on her. She'd lived that way long enough.

He waved her off. "They've got the routine down pretty good but don't expect five-star restaurant grub. It's more likely to be sloppy Joes.''

Given her limited cooking experience, the adolescents would probably do a better job than she could. Which didn't mean she couldn't learn. "I'll take over tomorrow, then.''

He frowned. "Whatever.'' He looked down at his shirtfront and started to unbutton it. "Meanwhile, I'm going to get out of this shirt before it starts to reek any more than it already does.''

"If you show me where things are, I can do the laundry.'' Not that she had any more experience at that chore than she did at cooking. Growing up in a house full of servants plus attending a string of boarding schools, she hadn't been highly motivated to develop her own domestic talents. But from necessity she had become acquainted with Laundromats during her college years.

"Not necessary. We've got it covered.''

And he didn't need her around mucking things up, she could almost hear him say.

She watched with curious fascination as he tugged his shirttail from his jeans, letting the shirt hang open.

A white V-neck T-shirt pulled tautly across his chest and she chided herself for the shimmer of regret that he wore an undershirt at all.

With a final, "We'll call you when supper's ready," he followed the rest of his cowhands into the sewing room to sort out the continuing bickering about the playpen—an easy-opening playpen she had managed with little effort the two nights she'd stayed in motels en route to Montana.

Smiling to herself, she walked around to the far side of the room and placed Suzanne on the bed. "We're going to be fine here, Susie-Q. You'll see. And it will only be for a short while, just long enough for me to decide what to do next."

When she looked up she saw Walker across the hall in his bedroom, the door standing open. He'd shed both his shirt and T-shirt, revealing a smooth back with well-defined muscles that rippled as he moved. His physique hadn't been built in the airless confines of an upscale gym somewhere in the middle of a big city, she realized, but by years of hard work on his ranch. He'd *earned* every sculpted inch of his lean body.

Elizabeth had never earned a damned thing, including her own keep. The best she'd done was work as an unpaid gofer for the charitable foundation her family supported. They'd offered her a small salary but she hadn't wanted to take money away from people who truly needed it.

With a raging sense of self disgust, she turned away

from the tempting view across the hall. Why on earth hadn't she noticed how stunted her life had become?

WALKER COULDN'T BELIEVE his eyes.

Every one of the boys was scrubbed clean and had their hair slicked back like a bunch of cowboys ready to whoop it up in town on Saturday night. Even Speed looked like he'd spiffed up for the evening. In this case, however, he suspected the sudden interest in cleanliness had more to do with their houseguest than the day of the week.

"You boys have supper ready?"

"Yes, boss," they chorused.

Lined up in front of the kitchen counter, they looked like soldiers standing at attention ready for inspection. They'd even hung their hats on the mudroom pegs, an event that only happened under the threat of dire punishment if they wore them while at the table.

"I made baked pork chops," Fridge announced.

"I did the mashed potatoes," Scotty added. "And the baked apples are in the oven now."

"I figured she might like some veggies." Bean Pole dipped his head. "My mom used to—when she was sober."

Walker glanced at Speed, who lifted his shoulders in an easy shrug. "Biscuits."

Apparently Walker was the only one who hadn't contributed to the meal preparations. He'd been searching out the current price of beef, a project that had been interrupted earlier. The news wasn't good. Evidently a lot of ranches were selling off their stock due to the drought, and the prices reflected a downward spiral.

He eyed the boys. "Well, are you gonna ask her to join us, or do you plan for us to eat it all ourselves?"

He'd seen a few stampedes in his life. But nothing like the boys jockeying for position as they raced out of the kitchen. For a moment, he thought Bean Pole was going to make it into the lead. No such luck, though. He bashed into a chair, spinning it around, allowing Scotty to squirt past him.

Shaking his head, Walker said, "It might be worth it to keep Lizzie around if it meant the boys would wash behind their ears more than once a year."

"That it would," Speed agreed. His weather-worn face shifted into a grin, and he looked far younger than his sixty-some years. "She is a pretty thing, ain't she?"

Walker wouldn't deny it. "She doesn't belong here." Not with her shiny long fingernails, her enticing scent or her designer jeans. Or the way she made him feel he'd been missing something.

"Cain't hurt the boys to have a female around for a while."

"I got along fine without a woman hanging over me all the time."

"If you say so, boss." Leaning back against the counter, Speed crossed his arms over his chest.

Walker's foreman had the most irritating way of telling him he was full of beans without saying a single damn word. He'd been doing that since Walker was a rebellious, snot-nosed fourteen-year-old who'd showed up at the Double O with no prospects and nowhere else to go. Sometimes Walker wondered if it had been Oliver Oakes who'd adopted him—or Speed. The answer was probably some of both.

A hushed sound came over the room. Almost magical.

Walker shifted his attention to the entrance to the kitchen, a swinging door he always propped open.

She'd spruced up, too, as if that were possible. She didn't look like any housekeeper he'd ever seen as she moved into the room as smoothly as a dancer arriving on stage. The summery dress she wore had a full skirt that floated at her knees, revealing calves that were both firm and smooth. The capped sleeves and scooped neck of her top showed off ivory skin that had rarely been blessed by the sun but looked just right for a man's caress.

Walker's hands ached to do just that, and he folded them into fists.

"Supper's ready." His throat had closed down so tightly, he was surprised he'd been able to speak.

"Yes, the boys told me." She smiled demurely.

Walker's reaction wasn't demure at all.

Behind her, her youthful entourage brought in the baby and her portable car seat, which they placed on a chair beside her. They hovered, groveling, hoping for some small crumb of attention, which she scattered among them bit by bit.

"Fridge!" Yanking out his own chair, Walker sat down, angry at himself because he wanted some of that attention to come his way. "Think you could serve supper sometime before we all pass out from hunger?"

Elizabeth watched in amazement as the boys exploded into action. A huge plate of pork chops appeared in the center of the big table, surely enough to feed the entire population of Grass Valley. The bowls of mashed potatoes and vegetables confirmed her belief that a hungry army of neighbors would be showing up at the door any moment. When Scotty produced a pan full of a dozen baked apples, the scent of cinnamon filling the room, and Speed added a mountain of steaming biscuits, she knew it had to be true.

With much chair scraping and jockeying for position, the boys took their places at the table. All eyes landed on her.

"It all looks delicious," she said, not quite sure what was expected of her. If she'd been at home, a servant would discreetly arrive, probably with a tureen of soup, and served her mother first then the rest of the guests. When that course was completed, her mother would ring a tiny bell and the servant would reappear to clear the bowls away.

Here *she* was supposed to be doing the cooking and serving, not sitting like a guest at the table.

"Why don't you help yourself, Lizzie?" Walker suggested. "The boys will pass you what you need."

She might be wrong but she still couldn't quite believe... "Shouldn't we wait for the rest of the guests?"

A puzzled look lowered his dark brows. "You're it as far as I know."

"You mean to tell me the six of us are going to eat all of that food?"

His grin softened the hard angles and planes of his rugged face, making him appear more approachable and more handsome. "Guess you haven't been around teenage boys much."

Returning his smile, she reached for the nearest serving dish, which was mounded high with mashed potatoes, a treat she hadn't allowed herself in years in an effort to watch her weight. "Hollow legs, I gather."

"Arms, legs, stomachs and sometimes their heads," Speed added, nudging Fridge with his elbow. "Help yourself, boys."

Passing Elizabeth each dish first before serving themselves, the boys demonstrated considerable self-restraint. If she hadn't known better, she would have thought she landed at an exclusive boarding school not a working ranch. Somehow she suspected they were all on their best behavior and that tickled her.

From the way Walker kept glancing around from his seat at the head of the table, she imagined he was surprised by the way the boys were acting, too—out of character for active adolescents.

"Are all of you boys from Montana?" she asked in the hope of getting them talking and therefore more at ease.

Fridge claimed Chicago and Scotty named Minnesota while Bean Pole remained shyly silent.

She tried a few more conversational gambits but the boys were either too busy eating or tongue-tied by her presence. It might take several days before they were entirely comfortable with her, she realized. Walker, too, unless he was always this quiet.

She'd only made it halfway through her gigantic meal when Suzanne started to fuss. Elizabeth picked her up.

"Looks like Susie-Q would like some dinner, too," she said. She scooted back from the table. "I'll get her bottle."

"Can I feed her?" Scotty asked. He jumped to his feet. "I used to feed my mom's baby, until they all moved away without me."

Elizabeth swallowed a gasp. The boy's *mother* had moved and left her child behind? What a dreadful—

"Feeding a baby's not so hard," Fridge said. "I could do it."

"Why don't we let Scotty do it this time?" Elizabeth suggested. She reached out and touched the boy with her hand. "And then later tonight you can have a turn, Fridge, if you're still interested."

Scotty looked pleased with himself and Fridge seemed grateful.

Softly, Bean Pole asked, "Could I feed her tomorrow?"

Feeling a band tighten around her chest, Elizabeth nodded. "Of course you may." These young men were so emotionally needy, it nearly broke her heart. They made her own problems pale by comparison. "Susie-Q is going to be in seventh heaven with all you boys paying her so much attention."

She glanced to the head of the table. An almost imperceptible nod from Walker told her she was doing the right thing by letting the boys help in the baby's care.

WITH THE BOYS FULLY ENGAGED in feeding Susie-Q, Walker and Speed were stuck doing the supper dishes.

"That was some dinner, wasn't it?" Walker commented as he rinsed a plate and slid it into the dishwasher.

"Yep. I thought there for a minute somebody had slipped us a whole bunch of new boys who knew how to use a fork right and kidnapped the old ones."

Walker chuckled. "Guess we'll have to have women out to the ranch more often so the boys can practice their manners."

"Sounds like a plan to me, long as they're as purdy as Miss Lizzie."

"That might be a little more difficult to arrange." He couldn't think of a single female in Grass Valley, married or not, who would match up with Lizzie. There probably wouldn't be all that many in Billings, for that matter.

After giving the table a final swipe with a damp cloth, Speed rinsed it out and laid it across the arm of the faucet.

"There's something I think you ought to know, boss."

"What's that?"

"Well, now, I'm not quite sure what it means but when we was getting Miss Lizzie's gear out of the trunk of her car, a box stuck in the back popped open." Thoughtfully, Speed ran his palm across his evening whiskers.

"And?" Walker prodded.

"Looked to me like there was a fancy wedding dress stuffed into the box. You know, all white lace and stuff."

Staring at his foreman, Walker tried to grasp the meaning of Speed's discovery.

Why in hell would a Merry Maids housekeeper travel from Nevada to Montana with a baby in the first place? And why would she have a wedding gown in the back of her car?

Heck of a thing to pack for a long trip. Or for scrubbing floors.

"What do you think?" Speed asked.

"I think I'd better have a chat with our housekeeper." And do it before some prospective groom showed up at his front door with a shotgun in his hand.

Chapter Three

Elizabeth knew the instant Walker entered the living room. It was as though he radiated a magnetic force that drew every eye in the room, most especially hers. She suspected he'd get the same reaction at a fancy charity ball in San Francisco as he did here, every woman drawn to him.

There was no sign of Speed, who she assumed must have gone to the bunkhouse after the kitchen cleanup. Or maybe even into town, such as it was with a business district no more than two blocks long.

Bean Pole, who was sitting awkwardly on a footstool in front of Scotty and the baby, complained, "Scotty won't let me and Fridge hold Susie-Q."

"She's asleep. You don't want to wake her, do you?" Scotty insisted, speaking softly but with an air of superiority as the resident expert on babies.

Deciding she needed to regain control of the parenting duties, Elizabeth rose from the couch. She felt Walker's appraising gaze and wondered what he was thinking. Men often found her attractive; she recognized the look. But she saw something else in

Walker's eyes that didn't bode well for her scheme—
the shadow of suspicion.

"Let's put Susie-Q back in the car seat," she said
to the boys. "She'll nap for a while and then will want
to play again before she goes down for the night."
She carried the car seat to a quiet corner of the room
out of the bright light, signaling Scotty to bring the
baby. "When she's ready for her last feeding, Fridge
can give her a bottle."

"Doesn't she eat any real food?" Bean Pole asked.

"Not yet. In another month I'll start her on cereal
and some vegetables."

The three adolescents formed a protective semicir-
cle around the baby, watching as though she were the
most fascinating thing in the world. Elizabeth agreed
with that assessment, of course. In the past three
months, she'd spent a good many hours observing
Suzanne in every situation imaginable. But to have
teenage boys find her baby equally intriguing surprised
her.

Lazily Walker strolled the rest of the way into the
room. "A watched pot never boils, boys."

Scotty glanced over his shoulder. "Huh?"

"I mean, you might as well relax and let the baby
sleep."

"Maybe there's wrestling on TV," Fridge suggested, glancing at the twenty-four-inch set strategi-
cally placed on a bookshelf near the fireplace.

Scotty gave him a thumbs-down on that idea. "The
noise would wake her up."

"No, it wouldn't," Fridge argued.

"You always start yelling 'n' stuff," Bean Pole said.

"You're the one who—"

Elizabeth winced as the bickering rose in volume. Insults were hurled. One shove became two, and she suddenly worried the wrestling match would take place right in the middle of the living room, putting Suzanne at risk of becoming an innocent victim.

But before she could take action, Walker intervened.

"That's it, boys." He didn't shout or react in anger. Even so, the adolescents responded instantly, freezing in midmotion, their mouths slamming shut. "Settle down or take it outside where it belongs."

Her admiration for Walker's ability to handle rambunctious teenagers kicked up a notch. Raised as she had been in a family where decorum reigned as gospel, she could barely imagine the day-to-day physicality of living with three adolescent boys. Yet Walker hadn't flinched. He was every inch a match for the three of them combined.

That thought gave her a little shiver of apprehension. Walker was so big, so strong, a woman would have no choice but to yield to his strength if he demanded it.

Yet, like the boys, she sensed an inner gentleness in Walker. A woman would have no reason to fear him, at least physically.

Protecting her heart would be a different matter.

SEVERAL HOURS LATER, arms folded across his chest, Walker leaned against the doorjamb of the sewing room watching Lizzie as she tucked the baby in for the night. A mighty pretty picture she created bending over the playpen but a puzzling one.

A woman with a wedding gown who wore no rings and acted like a debutante not a housekeeper.

The house was quiet now. The boys had gone back to the bunkhouse after lavishing attention on both Lizzie and the baby, hanging around the house until Fridge had his chance to give the ten o'clock bottle.

But the time had come for Walker to get down to business. He couldn't put off asking his questions any longer.

"The boys sure have taken a liking to you and the baby, Slick," he said.

Her head came up as though she'd forgotten he was there. "They're sweet. All of them."

"I usually describe them as ornery, rebellious and stubborn. Typical teenagers with pasts that haven't been easy."

She gave him a faint smile. "It's obvious you're doing a good job with them."

About twenty times a day he questioned both his sanity and whether he was doing right by the youngsters. Still, he did the best he could. He couldn't ask more than that of anyone.

Giving the baby a final caress, she stepped away from the playpen.

"Will she sleep through the night?" he asked.

"I hope so. But with so much excitement and being in a new place, it's hard to say."

He moved away from the door, and she followed him into the hallway where a low-wattage lightbulb cast muted shadows up and down the corridor, disguising the worn wallpaper and carpeting.

In contrast, Lizzie glowed with quiet vitality, her silver-blond hair shiny even in the dim light and her cheeks blooming with a trace of color. There hadn't been a woman living in this house in more than thirty years. Suddenly that felt wrong, almost as though the house had been incomplete all these years and no one had noticed.

Aware his thoughts were leading him in an unwanted direction, he cleared his throat. "You and I need to talk."

"It's been a long day and it's late. Would you mind if we waited until tomorrow? If Suzanne wakes up—"

"Tonight would be better. I don't want the boys interrupting us."

Her gazed flicked to his face for a moment, then she glanced back over her shoulder at the sleeping baby.

"Susie-Q will be fine," he said. "If she wakes up you'll be able to hear her downstairs."

"I wish you had a baby monitor."

"We've never had any need. Teenage boys can yell pretty loud."

She hesitated again. "Yes, I suppose so."

"We can talk in your bedroom, if you'd rather. Or mine."

With a quick shake of her head, Elizabeth rejected

both of those options. If she was going to be grilled by a sexy cowboy she didn't want to be anywhere near a bed. She was already far too aware of Walker's elemental maleness and the fact that they were alone in the house. She wasn't about to tempt fate.

She turned on her heel. "Downstairs will be fine." Her sandals slapped on the worn carpeting as she strode ahead of him. Now was the time to stay calm so she could keep her story straight. This was a perfect place to hide out. Except for the hum of tension she felt whenever Walker was near, the solitude of the ranch and the wide-open range were ideal for serious thinking.

And for learning how to be the woman she wanted to become.

Even the presence of the boys provided a sense of normalcy that would help her focus on what she wanted for her daughter's future and her own. Help her find the strength she needed to stand up to her family.

Walker was the only fly in the ointment. He was simply too unsettling for a woman's peace of mind.

She walked into the living room that was still strewn with baby equipment—Suzanne's car seat, a receiving blanket, the diaper bag—all of which she'd have to take upstairs. She started to gather them up.

"Speed tells me there's a wedding gown in the trunk of your car."

Her head snapped up. *Damn!* She'd forgotten all about the dress.

"Is that a problem?" she asked, faking a bland expression.

"Not unless a groom shows up here toting a shotgun."

"That's not likely to happen on my account."

"Why? Because there isn't a groom? Or he doesn't know where you are?"

Heat crept up her neck. Despite the current situation, she wasn't used to lying. It made her ill to her stomach. The pork chop she'd eaten for dinner did a roll in her midsection and threatened to do worse if she didn't come clean. Which she didn't dare. "What makes you think it's my gown?"

He eyed her skeptically. "Is it?"

"I was taking it to the cleaners' for my sister," she blurted out.

"Try again, Miss Thomas. People who are telling the truth don't blush."

The heat on her cheeks grew even more intense. "People who are being grilled by a great big lummox of a cowboy might do a lot of blushing."

He lifted his dark brows, etching his forehead with a double row of creases.

"I'm sorry. I didn't mean to insult you," she said. Wherever had her manners flown? Ever since she'd been able to walk and talk, her parents had drilled politeness into her head. Doing what was expected of her. Behaving properly. In the past three days she'd forgotten every lesson they'd taught her. Or more to the point, at the ripe old age of twenty-five, she'd finally decided to rebel against everything she'd ever known. To take charge of her own life—for Suzanne's sake as well as her own.

His lips quirked ever so slightly. "No insult taken. What I'm after is the truth."

Which was exactly what she couldn't tell him. Not yet. She didn't trust him enough for that. "If you'd like, you could call the Merry Maids corporate office to check my references."

"No one's likely to be around the office at eleven o'clock on a Saturday night."

"I suppose that's true."

Purposefully he walked over to the big native-rock fireplace, picked up the poker and jabbed at a charred log left over from the last fire. "I'd like to know what's going on now so I don't have to start making phone calls on Monday morning."

At least he wasn't threatening to call the police. So far.

Bending over, she scooped up Suzanne's blanket and stuffed it in the diaper bag, frantically trying to come up with a story Walker would buy. It's not like she had a whole lot of experience lying, a serious omission in her liberal-arts education, she now realized.

"Have you ever heard of the witness-protection program?" she ventured.

He stared at her with narrowed eyes but he didn't immediately dismiss her latest ruse. "Are you saying you witnessed a crime and are hiding out from the criminals?"

Perhaps with enough practice, she'd get prevarication down to a credible art form. "I'm not at liberty to discuss the details." And she really, truly didn't want to risk her family finding her just yet.

It was bad enough her hasty departure might place her family's ambition to see her brother Robert successfully launched in a political career in jeopardy without Vernon's support. She didn't want to deal with her guilt on that subject.

Sliding the poker back into its holder, Walker closed the fireplace screen and considered Lizzie's latest story. Assuming she really was from Nevada as her license plates suggested, he wouldn't be surprised if she'd come across a criminal element. Hadn't he heard about the mafia taking over Las Vegas? But he'd thought the state had cleaned up its act. Not that he paid much attention to any news that didn't involve the weather or the price of beef.

Maybe she had witnessed a crime. Or maybe she'd been scheduled to marry some mafia hit man and had run away at the last minute with her gown in the trunk.

But the way she still couldn't meet his gaze told him she'd lied to him again.

He walked over to the couch and picked up a cloth diaper she'd used for a spit-up rag, handing it to her.

"Have you broken the law?"

"Oh, no," she gasped. "Nothing like that."

For the first time, he believed her. Her response had been too quick, too insistent, to be a lie. He exhaled, surprised by the sense of relief he experienced.

"How 'bout Susie-Q? Is she really your baby?"

"Oh, my God! Did you think—of course she's my baby!"

He nodded. "I don't doubt it. She's got your smile."

"Don't you like babies?"

"I like 'em fine, I guess. But it seems to me, being a housekeeper and taking care of your baby at the same time wouldn't be easy." With each of her answers, he had new questions.

"I'm sure a lot of stay-at-home moms would agree with you."

"How about Susie's father?"

"He…he died." Her throat worked as though she were trying to tamp down her emotions. "About a year ago."

"I'm sorry. But are you telling me you've been driving around for a year with your wedding gown in the trunk of your car."

"No. I was going to marry someone else. It was a mistake and I…"

"You're not really a housekeeper, are you?"

She shook her head. "Not really. But I can learn, I'm sure of it." As though his interrogation had been too tiring, she sat down at the end of the couch and leaned back, closing her eyes in a gesture of defeat. "Are you going to send us away?"

A part of him knew that's exactly what he ought to do. If she really was in the witness protection system—which he didn't believe—the government should have been responsible for putting her in a safe place.

But whatever was happening, she was in some sort of trouble. A woman didn't run away with her baby on a whim, bridal gown or not. From what he'd seen of her, Lizzie was a good, loving mother. He gave her points for that.

But the fact that a groom had been left at the altar was troubling to say the least.

Even so, the irrational part of his brain argued that she should stay on the Double O for reasons that had nothing to do with the wedding gown, a groom or her baby—or any real or imagined witness-protection program—but simply because he wanted her here. Wanted the sultry scent of her to linger in a room after she left. Wanted to see the quick flash of her smile, even when it wasn't directed at him. Wanted to hope she wouldn't always be sleeping in the bed across the hall.

Damn it, he was getting ahead of himself. Sure, he lusted after her. She was a beautiful woman. But the truth of the matter was she and that little baby brought out his protective instincts. He couldn't turn away a person in trouble or in need. He had an idea she was both.

In frustration, he shoved his fingers through his hair. "You and Susie-Q can stay for now. But if you bring trouble down on the Double O, you're outta here. Is that understood?"

She lifted her head, her eyes a deep navy-blue and glistening with unshed tears. Slowly she pursed her lips then licked them. "Thank you," she whispered. "I promise you won't be sorry."

He already was sorry, but mostly because he didn't have the right to carry her upstairs and do with her what his libido had been demanding since she showed up in his driveway with her classy BMW, sophisticated airs and a chubby baby girl a man would be proud to call his own.

"Lizzie—"

"Yes?"

"Most of the boys who come here lie to me about one thing or another at first. Eventually they learn they can trust me. I hope you will, too."

She didn't answer. Instead she turned away, diaper bag in hand, and headed up the stairs.

He watched her go. Having Lizzie in the house was going to make changes in his life.

Including a hell of a lot of cold showers.

Chapter Four

Elizabeth snapped Suzanne into a clean jumper outfit and lifted the baby to her shoulder. She really could use a changing table. A proper crib, too, for that matter.

"Come on, Susie-Q. We're going to make breakfast for the boys." Surely, even blurry eyed from being up with her daughter three times during the night, Elizabeth would be able to pull together scrambled eggs and toast for a bunch of hungry cowboys. How hard could it be? And she wanted to start as soon as possible making herself useful around the house lest Walker think of an excuse to send her away.

Besides, if she intended to be an independent woman, she needed to start now by learning to do for herself and her baby. A housekeeping job—albeit an unpaid one—was a perfect opportunity.

She slipped Suzanne into the Snugli carrier she'd purchased in Reno, adjusting it so the baby was comfortable against her chest and her own hands were free to get some work done.

At a few minutes past six, she hurried downstairs

and found the kitchen empty, the only sign of life the coffeemaker with a freshly brewed pot on the warmer. Someone was up, probably Walker. And since the boys apparently hadn't arrived for breakfast yet, she'd have time to feed Suzanne, a task she dearly loved.

She quickly fixed a bottle, poured herself a cup of coffee and sat down at the table.

The kitchen was as big as the one in her parents' home, the appliances almost as new. But the old wooden table, scarred by use, gave it a homey feel missing in the glass and chrome version she'd grown up with.

Humming while Suzanne drank her formula and she sipped her coffee, a feeling of contentment swept over Elizabeth, more satisfying than she had felt in a long while. The months of wedding plans, not to mention her pregnancy and paralyzing grief over Steven's death, had taken its toll. The tension that had been plaguing her, making her shoulders ache and keeping her teeth on edge, eased away.

She sighed with relief.

The back door banged open, and she jumped at the sight of a stranger standing there. Tall and rangy with midnight-black hair, he had the distinctive features of a Native American.

"Well, now, looks like my brother has been keeping secrets from me." The smallest hint of a smile teased at the corners of his lips.

Her jaw went slack. Walker's *brother?* Except that both men were tall, there wasn't an iota of family resemblance.

When she continued to sit there mute, he strolled into the kitchen as if he owned the place. He tipped his hat to the back of his head. "I'm Rory, and you must be..." He left the question dangling, waiting for a response.

"I'm Eliz—ah, Lizzie Thomas. Walker's new housekeeper."

"His *housekeeper?*" He sputtered in surprise. "And your young friend?"

Elizabeth looked down at her daughter, who was dozing against her breast. She slipped the empty bottle from the baby's mouth and glanced up again at the stranger. "Suzanne. Walker calls her Susie-Q."

"He would. Can't seem to keep a person's name straight." With easy familiarity, he went to the cupboard, took down a mug and poured himself some coffee. "What does he call you? Besides Lizzie, I mean."

"Slick," she admitted.

He eyed her with intensely dark eyes. "My people named me Swift Eagle, so most of the time when we were kids, Walker called me Bird Brain."

She sputtered a laugh. "You're really brothers?"

"Yep. Me and Walker and another white-eyes named Eric were foster brats. Oliver Oakes adopted us."

She had no idea Walker had been in foster care, although that did explain his willingness to take in troubled youngsters now. "If you're looking for Walker, I'm not quite sure where—"

"He's out at the corral with the boys working a green horse."

"The boys are already up? It's only six-thirty."

"Oh, I imagine they've all been up since five. Walker runs a tight ship. I just came in for a cup of coffee. He has a couple of heifers with pinkeye he wanted me to check out."

So much for her grand plan to make herself useful. "They've probably already had breakfast, then." Which she had slept through.

"No doubt." Pulling out the chair next to her, he lifted a booted foot to the seat and rested a forearm across his thigh, mug still in hand. He leaned toward her. "Now tell me, Miss Lizzie Thomas, how does it happen my brother has all the luck when it comes to having a beautiful woman as a housekeeper?"

Despite the flush of pleasure his compliment brought, she suppressed a smile. "I'm not sure he sees me in that same light."

"I've always said he's somewhere between dumb and dumbest when it comes to women."

"I gather you and your brother have a loving relationship."

"*Blood* brothers. I bloodied his nose and he bloodied mine."

She couldn't help herself. She laughed out loud, startling Suzanne awake.

The back door opened again, admitting Walker in a rush of dry summer air. His Stetson was tipped back on his head, and he had the sleeves of his blue denim shirt rolled up as though the day had already turned warm.

"I'm sure glad I'm not paying you by the hour," he complained before coming to a complete halt. The rush of jealousy that whipped through his gut caught him entirely off guard. Why the hell was Rory *laughing* with Slick, happily on the receiving end of one of her most radiant smiles.

To top it off, she'd done something different with her hair. It was still pulled back, this time in a ponytail she'd double looped through an elastic scrunchy the same shade of blue as her eyes—a decorative addition he had an irritating urge to tug free in order that her hair would hang loose around her shoulders.

"In case you haven't noticed, big brother, you're not paying me at all. But if you'd like to, I'd be happy to send you an invoice."

"In your dreams," he muttered. To Lizzie he said, "I gather you've met Grass Valley's leading—and only, I might add—veterinarian."

"Yes. He tells me you're brothers. I must say, the family resemblance is…uncanny."

Walker scowled at his brother. They didn't look a damn bit alike.

"She's pulling your leg, boss man. I've been telling you for years, you've got to work on your sense of humor."

Ignoring his brother's remark, as he usually did, Walker centered his attention on Lizzie. "I'm glad you got to sleep late. I heard you up with the baby a couple of times. Restless night, huh?"

"I meant to be up in time to fix you and the boys breakfast. I'm sorry—"

"You don't have to do that," he said.

Swinging the chair back into its original position, Rory chuckled. "If you were my housekeeper, Miss Lizzie, trust me, I would have brought you breakfast in bed. As a welcome present."

"Yeah, and if I know you, it would have been dog chow," Walker countered. "Besides, don't you have something else to do instead of hanging around here?"

"You're right." Apparently unconcerned by his brother's jibes, Rory placed his mug on the counter. "They've got ringworm over at Riley's place. I'd best be going."

"It was nice to meet you, Rory," Lizzie said.

"My pleasure." He touched two fingers to the brim of his Stetson like some damn movie cowboy. "You let me know if this guy isn't behaving himself, all right? I'd always be happy to have company at my place."

Walker glared at his brother in a way meant to communicate Rory was trespassing on his territory. Which was ridiculous. Walker had no proprietary rights to Lizzie. She was a woman in trouble. He was simply helping out. Temporarily. If she wanted to hang around Rory's veterinary clinic, it was fine by him.

Or so he told himself.

When the outer door slammed shut behind Rory, Lizzie said, "I am sorry I didn't get up in time to help with breakfast."

"There was no need. We're pretty self-sufficient around here."

Holding Susie-Q in her lap, she patted the baby's back. Drool edged out of the corners of her mouth. "I do want to be helpful while I'm here."

Which Walker didn't imagine would be long. He didn't run a dude ranch and there wasn't a decent mall in a hundred miles, much less a place to get her siren-red nails fixed if she broke one.

"The boys are on their own to rustle up their own lunches. But they'd probably enjoy a woman's cooking for supper, if you're willing."

"I could probably put together a nice salad for dinner, if you have the fixings. I always lose my appetite in hot weather, don't you?"

He narrowed his eyes. "Slick, remember we're talkin' about boys with hollow legs. It takes something solid to fill them up."

"Yes, of course, I wasn't thinking—"

"They like fried chicken. You think you could handle that?"

"I, well, fried chicken sounds fine." Elizabeth glanced around the kitchen in the desperate hope of spotting a cookbook. Surely in one of the cupboards she'd find—

"When you're finished with breakfast, come on out. I'll give you a tour of the place."

"I'd like that, thank you."

He gave her an odd look she couldn't interpret, then went out the back way, leaving her wondering why he'd come in the house at all. And why he'd acted so funny toward his brother, Rory.

"Miss Susie-Q." She lifted the baby up in the air. "We have our work cut out for us if we're going to persuade Mr. Walker Oakes that he hasn't made a mistake by letting us stay."

She'd always worried about what others thought of her. Indeed, she'd made friends easily over the years, largely because she went along with what they wanted. And, of course, her family was influential, which drew people to her, often asking for favors. Few in the business community wanted to cross her father and no woman in the country-club set would think of going up against her mother in a dispute. Growing up, Elizabeth had the protection of her family wrapped around her like a security blanket.

In Montana she was on her own. She'd have to prove her worth to others—and, more importantly, to herself.

Getting up from the table, she braced Suzanne with one arm and started opening cupboard doors. "We'll do just fine, Susie-Q. Assuming I can find a cookbook."

"WHAT A GLORIOUS DAY." Standing at the corral fence, Suzanne snuggled next to her chest, Elizabeth looked up at a clear-blue sky. Not a single cloud dotted the horizon, not even beyond the rolling, tree-covered hills to the west. Although it was still early, the temperature was beginning to climb and would likely reach eighty before long.

"It would be better if we got rain," Walker mumbled.

"And ruin a perfectly good day at the beach? No way."

His head snapped around. "The beach is about a thousand miles west, in case you hadn't noticed."

"It's a manner of speaking." Tossing her head, she strolled along the corral fence until she reached the sorrel the boys had been working. "I bet you'd like to go for a run in the surf, wouldn't you, sweetie?"

"Careful," Walker warned. "She's still green. There's no predicting—"

"She's fine, aren't you, honey bunch?" She stroked the horse's velvety nose and scratched her cheek with her fingernails. "You're just a little agitated by all those boys."

"You know about horses?" Walker seemed as surprised as though she'd announced she were an expert volcanologist.

"I've owned several," she said primly, before realizing she should have bitten her tongue before admitting to any such thing. She didn't dare give him a clue as to who she really was—a woman who was hiding out from family pressures she couldn't handle.

"Where?"

"Why does it matter? Horses don't have a very good sense of geography." Turning away from the sorrel, she forced herself to meet Walker's skeptical gaze. "You said you were going to show me around."

"Not that there's a whole lot to see that would interest a city slicker."

"Try me, cowboy."

A megawatt of electricity zapped between them as they both realized the double meaning of her words.

"I didn't mean—"

"Of course not." His lips canted into a grin with fully as many watts as the Grand Coulee Dam produced. "Barns and fields of hay are really exciting."

Not willing to let him get the upper hand, she said, "With the right tour guide, I'm sure they'll be fascinating."

He sputtered. Amazingly his tanned cheeks took on a rosy hue as though he were embarrassed by a little harmless flirtation. "You need a hat on if you're going to be out here in the sun."

"I didn't think to bring one with me."

"In a hurry to leave home, were you?"

"You could say that."

He studied her for a moment, his expression again unreadable, then he shouted to one of the boys. "Bean Pole, bring me that straw hat I keep in the barn."

The young man's head poked out of the barn. "Comin'!"

Seconds later the youngster appeared, Bandit bounding along beside him. The boy handed her the most bedraggled straw hat Elizabeth had ever seen and gave her a shy smile before running off again. Bandit took time to sniff around her legs before racing after the boy.

Holding the hat in her hand, she eyed Walker skeptically. "I wouldn't want to deprive your local scarecrow of his crowning glory."

"In Kansas they've got scarecrows. Not here."

"Then this is—" delicately, she placed the hat on her head "—a fashion statement?"

A potent smile transformed his expression from stern to dynamite sexy. "Montana style."

ELIZABETH NOTED THE BARN sported a fresher coat of red paint than the white that covered the house, suggesting Walker's priorities were focused on the workings of the ranch, not his living accommodations.

The barn door mawed open, the shadowed interior revealing a huge tractor far more modern than the one that appeared abandoned beside the barn. Inside were all of the accoutrements for a big operation, from horse stalls and a tack room with a dozen bridles and saddles to tilling disks for the tractor.

"How big a ranch do you have?" she asked, enjoying the rich scents of horses and hay as they brought back fond memories of her youthful equestrian efforts.

He shrugged negligently. "About three thousand acres. Every time some land became available in the valley, my dad snapped it up."

"Very impressive."

"The hard part is keeping it all running without going so far in debt that the bank ends up owning it all, lock, stock and tractors."

"Which can't be easy with the price of beef slipping."

He slanted her a surprised look from beneath his Stetson. "How do you know about the price of beef?"

"I've been known to read a newspaper now and then."

His lips twitched ever so slightly. "Now why hadn't I thought of that?"

The man was so potent, even with only the hint of a smile, Elizabeth wondered how he'd managed to remain single so long. Every woman in Montana should have been after him, matrimony on her mind. Not that Elizabeth intended to follow suit. She had her own agenda for being in Montana, which didn't include developing a relationship with a long-legged, lean-hipped cowboy with a wickedly sexy smile he seemed reluctant to use.

They strolled back outside, and Elizabeth found herself squinting despite the straw hat. She lifted a flap on the Snugli carrier to shade Suzanne's eyes, too.

"That's the calving barn," Walker said, pointing out a low building with metal gates partitioning off several stalls.

"You bring your cows in off the range when they're having their calves?"

"When we can. The calves do better if we give them a couple of days to get their feet under them before letting them out on their own. Of course, if there's a late spring blizzard, we may not even be able to get to them with a load of hay much less any shelter."

"Which means you lose the calf."

"Sometimes the mother, too, if she's too weak to graze or the snow's too deep for her to get to the grass."

"Sounds like being a successful cattle rancher takes a lot of luck."

"And hard work. This is unforgiving country."

She detected a note of warning in his voice—*this is no place for wimps or city slickers.* Fortunately she'd decided to no longer be a wimp. She couldn't do much about being a city girl. That's where she'd been raised. Or more accurately, in boarding schools with rolling green lawns, well-tended flower beds and architecturally drab buildings covered with ivy.

As they strolled along, Fridge rode up on a chestnut quarter horse, coming smartly to a halt in front of Walker and tipping his hat to Elizabeth.

"Morning, Miss Lizzie." He smiled down at her, so proud of his horsemanship he was about to burst with it.

"Good morning, Fridge. You boys certainly get up early."

"Yes, ma'am. There's lots of work to be done on a ranch. The boss here couldn't do it all alone."

She stifled a smile. "I'm sure that's true."

"Seems to me that's what you ought to be doing, son," Walker said. "Working."

"Uh, yes, sir, I already fed the horses. But Speed said to tell you the salt lick on the west section is about wore down. Says we ought'a get a new one when we're in town."

"Thank you for that message. I'll take care of it."

Looking disappointed that he hadn't been asked to linger, he tipped his hat again, reined his horse around and galloped off.

Walker shook his head. "I swear those boys aren't likely to get a lick of work done while you're around but their manners sure have improved."

"I imagine, given enough time, they'll get used to me."

Tucking his fingers in his hip pockets, Walker didn't think it would be easy for any man to get used to Lizzie being around. Even wearing his beat-up old hat, she looked like a Thoroughbred compared to other women he'd known. If she'd been taller he would have guessed she was a model or maybe a Vegas dancer. But since she only came up to his chin, he figured her for a socialite.

Meanwhile, Lizzie wearing those jeans ought to be against the law. They gave a man too many ideas, all of them guilty as sin.

Anxious to direct his thoughts elsewhere, he said, "Not much else to see around here. The bunkhouse is over there and behind that is the chicken coop. You wanna go pick out a chicken or two to fry up for supper? We've got a real sharp ax."

She gasped. "You expect me to kill and butcher—"

"Pluck 'em, too. That's what we do on a ranch, when we're not slaughtering a steer, of course."

"Oh, I don't think I can…I mean, I've never…" She'd paled so badly her porcelain skin had turned nearly white. "I couldn't kill anything, really I couldn't."

Mentally he kicked himself. God, he was worse than the boys, more adolescent in the way he wanted to tease her. Like he'd been as a sixth-grader, tugging a girl's ponytail because he didn't know what else to do with his raging hormones.

"Hey, I'm pulling your leg, Slick. I wouldn't ask you to do that. Besides, the chickens I've got are layers, not fryers. I keep them for the eggs. Scotty's job is to gather them every morning." He wouldn't mention when summer was over he'd slaughter the hens. There wasn't a warm enough place to keep the chickens during the winter months except inside the house, and he drew the line at that.

Whirling, she nailed him a look with enough blue fire to melt an iceberg. "Was that a test you just gave me?"

Probably. One that *he'd* failed. "Of course not."

"Good." She sniffed and raised her chin a notch. "*You* can kill the chicken."

He grinned. "There's some in the freezer."

"What?"

"Chickens. Legs, breasts, wings. Bought at the grocery store."

Some of the steam went out of her fury. "Well, then, I suppose I ought to go defrost them if we're going to eat tonight."

"That would be good," he agreed, thoroughly chastised and ashamed of himself.

She held his gaze steadily. "I don't suppose there is a deli in Grass Valley that delivers."

"Not likely."

"I was afraid of that."

He watched her turn and walk back toward the

house, her hips shifting gracefully with each step she took as though she were a fashion model taking a stroll down the runway. *His housekeeper wants to know if there's a deli that delivers?* Not in his world.

Which was another reason Lizzie Thomas didn't belong here.

And he hated like hell that she didn't.

"Hey, Slick," he called to her.

She glanced over her shoulder.

"I was planning to take the boys into town for church. Why don't you come with us? We'll eat in town and you can do the chicken tomorrow night."

She seemed to weigh her decision for a long time before finally nodding. "Yes, I'd like that. Thank you for inviting me."

Walker had the troubling feeling the wedding gown in the back of Lizzie's BMW was the reason it had taken her so long to make up her mind. She wanted to avoid any chance of crossing paths with the would-be groom.

For that matter, so did Walker.

Chapter Five

Elizabeth watched the scenery fly by as Walker barreled his pickup along a narrow two-lane highway. In the extended cab seat behind her, Suzanne was strapped in, Scotty dutifully watching over her. She'd promised Bean Pole he could ride with the baby on the way home. For once, Fridge hadn't argued, happier riding in Speed's truck where he had more room.

Outside, clusters of black and brown cattle dotted rolling countryside rarely broken by the presence of a tree and no sign at all of habitation. Walker's nearest neighbor must literally be miles away. Even on her parents' large estate, the neighbors were only a few hundred feet away, crowded conditions by Montana standards.

"Is all of this land yours?" she asked.

Walker glanced toward her. For church he'd changed into a dressy Western-style shirt in an ivory color that set off his deep tan and was wearing a bolo tie with a polished stone the same shade of bronze as his eyes. Not that he'd looked bad before, but he'd certainly cleaned up real good.

"The land on the right is Double O. The Bar-X owns from the road south to town. Dad tried to buy out Harry Morgan a couple of times but the old guy wouldn't go along."

"Is he your nearest neighbor?"

"As the crow flies, I suppose. It's a long way around to the entrance of his ranch. Unless you want to go across country, you have go through town to get there."

"Do you and the boys ever get lonely so far away from the rest of the world?"

"The Double O *is* my world, Slick." *His* world but not *hers*, his tone reminded her.

He was right, of course. Her eagerness to accept a reprieve from cooking dinner was a sure sign of that. Despite her fear she'd have to mix with strangers who would ask too many questions, she'd agreed to go into town.

With luck, she'd dodge the most awkward questions and maybe even find a grocery store with bake-at-home pizzas to tide her over until she could get some help in the culinary department. In her search for a cookbook she'd come up empty.

Scattered houses on one- and two-acre lots appeared as the highway dipped toward the Sage River, and they approached the town. Across the river, pine trees inched their way up the hillside until they covered the slopes in a deep, rich green.

The town itself offered little to brag about—a garage with an assortment of ancient, disreputable cars parked all around it, a general store carrying both dry goods and groceries, a drugstore with a neon outline of an ice-cream cone above the door, and a coffee shop with a big plate glass window still decorated for Christmas. Based on the number of cars parked out front, the two busiest places in town were the Grass Valley Saloon—featuring Good Eats according to the wind-tattered banner—and the church across the street.

Walker pulled into the church parking lot with Speed right behind them.

Modest by any standards, the small church sported a bright coat of whitewash, a flower bed in colorful bloom and a bell tower topped with a lightning rod. Pickup trucks of all ages, most of them with dinged fenders and rusty truck beds, crowded the parking lot. With ranches scattered so far apart, attending church had to be the major social occasion of the week.

Elizabeth suddenly got a bad case of the bashfuls as she climbed down from Walker's truck. The folks who were hurrying into the church were his friends. She didn't belong here, not while masquerading as someone she wasn't.

"Maybe I should have stayed at the ranch," she began as Walker handed Suzanne to her. Scotty had already run off with friends his age. Fridge, she noted, had fallen into step beside a slender young girl who looked to be about sixteen and had smiled sweetly at him. Bean Pole tagged along behind them.

"You'll be fine," Walker assured her. He grabbed the diaper bag from the floor of the back seat. "These folks won't bite."

"What are you going to say when they ask—"

"You're my housekeeper. That will be good enough for them."

"You've had a lot of housekeepers, have you?"

"It's not like you're the first stranger I've brought with me to church."

But the first woman? she wondered. "Have you ever been married?"

He halted abruptly. "No."

"Ever come close?"

His forehead pleated into a frown. "Let's get inside. The service is about to start."

Granted she'd been prying into Walker's private life, but she found it interesting he'd evaded her question.

Just as she'd evaded his.

She felt the curious stares as they entered the church together and walked down the side aisle, forced by the crowded pews to sit near the front. Women craned their necks to look at her, men gave Walker knowing nods. All the while, Elizabeth's cheeks flushed as though she'd been out in the sun for hours.

Darn it all! If she'd known how to cook a decent meal, she wouldn't have gotten herself into this mess.

She didn't hear much of the sermon. Only a few minutes into the service, Suzanne woke up and started to fuss. The woman next to her smiled indulgently, offering to hold the baby, but Elizabeth elected to give her a bottle. Which, from the perspective of the poor lady sitting behind her, turned out to be a serious mistake.

Elizabeth had lifted Suzanne to her shoulder to burp

her at the precise moment the preacher asked everyone to stand for the doxology. The lady behind her leaned forward right on cue, and Susie-Q did her giant, juicy burp.

"Oh, I'm so sorry," Elizabeth said in a hushed voice, shifting around in the pew to offer a cloth to wipe up the mess.

"It's all right, dear. Not the first time some little rascal has made a fright of my Sunday best." The gray-haired lady brushed at her skirt with the cloth. "In fact, my Daryl didn't outgrow the problem till he was almost two. I stopped worrying about the stains."

Elizabeth nearly groaned aloud. If only she hadn't agreed to Vernon's demand she stop breast-feeding Suzanne. *Next* time, if there ever was one, she'd know better.

THE MOMENT WALKER STEPPED out of the church, he fully realized what he'd gotten himself into by bringing Lizzie to the service. Every woman in town with a wagging tongue and an insatiable appetite for gossip surrounded them.

"What a dear little baby," Hetty Moore, the owner of the general store cooed. "We're so pleased you brought this young lady to church, Walker, dear."

"Yes, ma'am." He made a hasty introduction but before he was finished he had to include Dr. Justine Beauchamp, who had given him more tetanus and antibiotic shots than he cared to remember. He swore his brother Rory used smaller needles on the horses he treated.

"Will you be staying with Walker long?" Hetty asked.

"I'm not quite sure," Lizzie answered smoothly, "but I was hoping to stop by the general store this afternoon."

"Oh, no, dear, we're closed on Sundays. The sabbath, you know."

Lizzie's smile stayed in place, but Walker could see she was upset. He wondered what she'd hoped to buy. He had most everything she'd need at the ranch—except special things a woman might need.

"Have you known Walker long?" the doctor asked. "Or is it one of the boys—"

"If you'll excuse me," Lizzie said. "Suzanne had a bit of an upset tummy in church, and I think I'd better get her home."

"Of course, you run along, dear," Hetty said. "Be sure to come again. We have a potluck after service next week."

"If you need me to have a look at the baby, just call," Doc Justine offered.

"I'm sure she'll be fine."

Lizzie slid away from the women as smoothly as a muskrat slips into a quiet pool for a swim. Not a ripple marred the calm surface as the two ladies wished her well.

Walker had to hurry to catch up. "How'd you learn how to do that?"

"Do what?"

"Turn up your nose to those women without them

realizing what you were doing. Hetty can usually get a stone to talk.''

She opened the truck door and looked over her shoulder at him, her eyes glistening with mirth. ''Years and years of finishing schools.'' Lifting the baby from her carrier, she laid Susie-Q down on the seat to change her.

Walker shook his head. *Finishing school!* Damn, he should have known that.

Chalk up one more reason why Slick would never last on an isolated ranch in northern Montana.

A big hand closed over Walker's shoulder.

''Hey, Sharp Shooter, what's your hurry?''

Wincing, Walker turned to greet his brother, Eric. ''Trying to avoid the law, what else?''

Smiling, Eric looked past him to Lizzie. ''More likely you're trying to avoid introducing me to this pretty young lady. Rory called to tell me you'd hired a housekeeper. Gettin' pretty uppity, aren't you, Sharpy?''

Walker silently cursed having two brothers who couldn't keep their respective noses out of his business. ''Lizzie, this is my other brother, Sheriff Eric Oakes. About the only thing he's good for around here is to lock up folks with overdue library books.''

Demurely she smiled and extended her hand. ''I gather you don't have much crime in Grass Valley.''

''I've scared off all the hard-core criminals, ma'am, to make the town safe for the fairer sex.''

''I'm sure we're all grateful, Sheriff.''

When Eric didn't immediately let go of Lizzie's

hand, Walker elbowed him out of the way. "You gotta watch out for this guy, Slick. He plays with handcuffs."

She sputtered a laugh. "I'll be sure to remember that."

What Walker remembered the most was the way he and his brothers had vied for girlfriends over the years. Mostly the competition had been a draw.

For some reason, Walker had the unreasonable urge not to lose this time.

"You two and the boys going to eat at the saloon today?" Eric asked.

"I was thinking about it," Walker admitted. In fact, that had been his plan, although he wished he could come up with a better one at the moment—one that didn't include sharing Lizzie with his brother.

"Great." Eric's smile was as wide as a Montana sky. "I'll join you."

Lizzie spent a few moments changing Susie-Q's diaper, then they headed across the street. Halfway there she angled him a look. "I wouldn't think of interfering between brothers, but what's this about Eric calling you Sharp Shooter?"

Damn! He should have known she'd pick up on that.

He forced a shrug. "Shortly after I arrived at the Double O I decided to show off how good I was with a rifle. Not that I'd ever shot one before but I was pretty full of myself. I found the key to Dad's locked cabinet and took one of his rifles, determined to get myself a deer and show everybody what a great hunter I was.''

''Somehow I don't think this story is going to end happily,'' Lizzie said.

''He was damn lucky he didn't kill himself,'' Eric commented.

''It was only a flesh wound,'' Walker grumbled.

Lizzie turned her head away but not before he saw the beginnings of a smile. Hell, it was funny, not that it had been at the time. And he'd been told by more than one woman that the scar on his thigh made him look heroic.

Of course, he hadn't always admitted the scar was the result of something stupid he'd done. A wound inflicted by a marauding mountain lion sounded a lot better.

MONDAY MORNING ELIZABETH got down to business. She'd enjoyed her meal at the Grass Valley Saloon, despite her concern they were serving minors where alcohol was available. No one else appeared worried, however, including the local sheriff. And she'd had one of the best, most cholesterol-filled hamburgers imaginable. She'd be dieting for days to get rid of the weight she was sure she'd gained.

But her respite was over. Making dinner for five hungry men loomed large on the horizon.

''Yes, I'd like both of those cookbooks you mentioned.'' Elizabeth cradled the phone on her shoulder as she talked to the bookstore owner she'd called long distance, taking notes. ''I wonder, could you just check to be sure there's a recipe for fried chicken in that *Cooking, Quick and Easy* book?''

Pages rustled while the bookstore owner flipped through the book.

"Under fried chicken there are recipes for Virginia battered fried, deep fried, oven fried—"

"Let's try oven fried." That sounded the easiest. "Could you read the recipe to me, please."

More pages rustled. "Let's see, four pounds of chicken parts—"

Elizabeth wrote as fast as she was able, thinking she'd triple the recipe. She could do this. Cooking couldn't be any more difficult than chemistry class— where she'd blown up a test tube containing a sulfur compound, she recalled with more than a little chagrin. The entire boarding school had been evacuated for the rest of the day. Her classmates had loved her.

"That's wonderful," she said when the store owner reached the end of the recipe. "I really appreciate your help."

"My pleasure. Now, did you want both of these cookbooks or just the one?"

"Both, please. I'd like them shipped special overnight delivery, C.O.D."

"Oh, dear. There'll be an extra charge for that and they only take cash."

"Not a problem. As you may suspect, the situation is quite urgent." A true crisis, in Elizabeth's view, since she'd searched the entire household and hadn't come up with a single cookbook to see her through even one meal, much less however many days or weeks she hoped to stay at the Double O Ranch.

"Very well then. I'll have the books out to you this afternoon."

"Bless you." Walker, Speed and the boys would no doubt bless the bookstore owner as well.

As soon as she hung up, she placed another call. While the need for a baby monitor, changing table and a crib might not be as urgent as the cookbook, she saw no reason to delay. She planned to be here for a while. She intended Suzanne be both safe and comfortable.

Fighting a niggling sense of guilt, she tried not to think about the possibility that her own heart might not be safe in such close proximity to Walker Oakes.

FOR THE THIRD DAY IN A ROW the boys had scrubbed their faces and hands and put on clean shirts for supper. It was a habit Walker ought to encourage. But it irritated him the reason for their sudden interest in cleanliness was Lizzie, not his own edicts, which often fell on deaf ears.

The fact that he'd changed his shirt, too, only further annoyed him. Lizzie was making inroads into his life that wouldn't be easily erased when she left.

"That chicken looks terrific," Speed said, carrying the heaping platter from the stove to the table. The boys were all standing around, waiting expectantly.

Lizzie's cheeks were flushed from the heat of the oven and her usually neat hair clung damply to her neck in flaxen strands. She was wearing a summery blouse and skirt and sandals. She'd managed to splash something on her blouse and the baby had dribbled down her back. The way Susie-Q kept fussing compounded Lizzie's frazzled appearance. She tried to soothe the baby but to no avail.

"Let me take her," Walker said.

Lizzie looked up at him gratefully. "I don't know what's wrong with her. She only had a half-hour nap this afternoon and she won't go back down for me." She handed the baby to Walker. "As soon as I get dinner on the table, I'll take her upstairs—"

The moment Susie-Q slid in his hands, she went as still as a mouse, gazing up at him with big, blue eyes. She didn't weigh all that much, not much more than a ten-pound sack of sugar, and he settled her in the crook of his arm. The motion caused her to giggle, and she gave him a toothless grin.

Something inside Walker eased, a tangled knot of anger that had been hiding there since he was a kid when his mother had left him in a grocery store while she drove off with her new husband. The sensation was almost painful, as though he'd stretched a muscle he hadn't used in a long time, and he smiled back at the infant.

"Trying to get on my good side, are you?" he said. His reward was another drooling, toothless smile that gave him the same feeling inside, a spreading warmth that relaxed years of hidden tension.

"You appear to have the magic touch," Lizzie said.

"She wouldn't stop crying for me," Scotty admitted. "Not even when I made funny faces at her."

Wiping the drool away from her lips with his fingertip, Walker said, "Maybe she prefers an older man."

"You all sit down," Lizzie ordered, "while I get dinner on the table. This golden moment of silence may not last."

Oddly Walker wanted it to. Not so much because he wanted Susie-Q to quit crying but because she felt comfortable cradled in his arm. Granted it had taken a couple of days for him to get used to having a baby around. But now, with her wide eyes, button nose and captivating smile, he couldn't remember why he'd been so nervous. Holding her wasn't nearly as hard as wrestling a newborn calf, and they didn't smile back at you.

The boys bolted for their chairs while Speed helped Lizzie put the rest of the food on the table.

"I couldn't figure out how to make biscuits so you'll have to eat bread," she said.

"Bread's fine with me," Fridge said, already reaching for the plate of bread on the table and the butter dish.

"And I was going to put together a three-bean salad but I could only find two kinds in the pantry."

Speed slid the big bowl of beans on the table. "The boys aren't real fussy about their beans, are you, boys?"

"Not me," Fridge agreed.

"Like you're fussy about any kind of food," Scotty commented.

Walker eyed the dish of mashed potatoes Lizzie removed from the oven to put on the table, not exactly creamy looking and an odd shade of beige. Probably some fancy dish she'd eaten at a ritzy restaurant.

Rounding out the meal, Elizabeth put a bowl of chopped apples, raisins and nuts on the table—her attempt at a Waldorf salad—and said a little prayer everything would taste all right. She didn't like the way the apples had browned around the edges but surely they hadn't spoiled so quickly.

Wiping her hands on a towel, she reached for the baby. "Here, let me take Susie-Q back so you can eat."

"Let's not rock the boat. For the moment, at least, she seems happy enough."

"If you're sure."

"She and I are coming to an understanding, aren't we, Susie-Q? She hasn't spit up on me for a full five minutes."

Exhausted as she was from fixing dinner, Elizabeth smiled and a band tightened around her heart. Walker looked like a gentle giant holding Suzanne, the baby looking up at him with adoration in her eyes.

Her baby needed a father. Someone who was patient, a man she could trust as she grew from infant to toddler and finally from adolescent to young woman.

She'd lost Steve and knew Vernon would never be that man. Elizabeth was more confident of that now than she had ever been. But Walker hadn't volunteered for the job, either. She'd tricked him into letting them stay. Pleaded, actually, without telling him the entire truth about herself—or the politically influential man she'd been scheduled to marry.

Leaving Vernon standing almost literally at the altar wouldn't do a thing for her brother Robert's political ambitions.

As Walker gingerly shifted his chair and sat down, Suzanne still snuggled in the crook of his arm, tears of regret prickled at the backs of Elizabeth's eyes. Being here was only temporary, a refuge she'd sought until she could stand on her own two feet.

And then she'd have to leave.

Platters and bowls circled the table as the boys served themselves, heaping their plates and passing the dishes along. As well mannered as her first night at the ranch, they waited for Elizabeth to take a bite.

She stabbed a green bean and kidney bean together and forked them into her mouth. Instantly her lips puckered.

"Oh, dear, I must have put too much vinegar on the beans." She'd been so sure that was how a three-bean salad was made.

The boys eyed each other across the table. Finally Fridge had the courage to try the beans.

He ventured a bite and his eyes watered. "Hey, these are great. They've got a little zing to them, that's all," he said, reaching for his glass of milk.

Bless his heart! He was trying to make her feel better.

The other boys followed suit. They gagged down a bean or two, then gulped some milk.

"You don't have to eat them," she said.

"They're great," Scotty and Bean Pole chorused, but she noticed they both tried the Waldorf salad next.

Tentatively she tasted the chicken. More coating had stuck to the pan than the chicken legs but the flavor was all right. At least the meat was cooked through.

Delicately Bean Pole removed something from his mouth. He dropped it to his plate with a *clink.* "I think I just broke a tooth."

From her salad? Oh, dear—

Something *clinked* onto Scotty's plate. "Me, too."

Elizabeth leaned over to look at the boy's plate. "That's not your tooth. That's a raisin."

Walker cleaned his throat. "You find those way in the back of a cupboard?"

"I had to stand on a chair to reach them."

"They're, uh, pretty old. I guess that's why they're so hard."

She sighed. "Well, the apples ought to be okay."

"Yes, ma'am," Fridge agreed, neatly picking out the apples with his fork.

With her first bite of mashed potatoes, she realized she'd blown that dish, too. They were as dry as toast with lumps the size of golf balls. Her chin quivered. "I'm sorry. I scorched the potatoes. I never should have tried fixing—"

"It won't hurt the boys to experience something different for a change," Walker said. "And besides, the chicken's great. Isn't it, guys?"

"You bet." Fridge reached halfway across the table for another chicken leg.

She could only hope she'd cooked enough chicken to fill them up. The rest of the meal wasn't fit for pigs. Unfortunately Walker didn't raise any of those. And darn it all, he was being so sweet, he probably would have gone out and bought one if she suggested it. Who knew such a big, tough cowboy would have such a soft heart?

When dinner was thankfully over, Speed and the boys got up to clear the table.

"I'll do that," she said. "It's the least I can do after the disastrous meal I tried to feed you."

Walker was still holding Suzanne, who was sound asleep. "Let them do it," he said. "You go rest in the living room and I'll bring Susie-Q in there."

Too weary to argue, she did as he asked. Given the fiasco of her domestic efforts so far, she'd probably break the dishwasher anyway. Why on earth hadn't she paid more attention to Isabel Sword, the cook her family had employed for more years than she could remember?

She collapsed onto the couch, and Walker sat down opposite her. Suzanne appeared to have taken up permanent residence in his arms, and she was damn jealous. Which proved exactly how tired she was.

"You might want to try a little milk with the potatoes next time."

"Milk?"

"Butter and salt are good, too."

"Oh. I didn't know."

"Don't worry about it."

His kindness brought tears to her eyes again. "I'll do better tomorrow." After the cookbooks arrived.

Thank heavens she'd ordered them for overnight delivery.

Chapter Six

Walker met the delivery truck when it pulled up in front of the house. It was before noon on yet another cloudless day. Even the Sage River was beginning to dry up, they'd been so long without rain. Every day the land grew more parched, thirsty for the refreshing taste of water.

"Hey, Walker, how's it going?" Pete Williams, the driver, worked out of Havre, traveling miles every day to cover a huge delivery district. "Big order today."

"Can't be for me. Speed must have ordered something."

"Your name's on the packages."

Packages? Thumbing his hat to the back of his head, Walker frowned. For the life of him, he couldn't remember ordering a thing in the past several months.

Electronic clipboard in hand, Pete hopped down from the truck. "They're all C.O.D. The total comes to $872.53."

Walker nearly choked. "There's got to be some mistake. I didn't order—"

The door on the front porch burst open and Lizzie

came hurrying outside. Despite her rush, she moved with the smooth grace of clear water flowing through a mountain stream. "Oh, I'm so glad you got here so early."

Pete's eyes widened. "Gee, I didn't know you got married, Walker. Congratu—"

"I haven't. She's my new housekeeper." A woman who still hadn't been entirely honest with him.

"I hope you brought everything I ordered," she said.

"*You* ordered?" Walker questioned.

"Six items, ma'am."

"That sounds perfect." She reached for the clipboard to sign for the delivery.

"What the hell did you order?"

"I decided Susie-Q needed a proper crib, and then I can use the playpen downstairs for her to nap in while I'm busy down there. And we talked about a baby monitor. When she's upstairs, I want to be able to hear—"

"Do you have any idea how much all that stuff costs?"

She gave him a blank look. "I didn't actually add it up."

"Nearly a thousand dollars! I don't have anywhere near that kind of cash around the house." Hell, he didn't have a whole lot more than that in the bank.

"Oh, I'm going to pay for it." She looked surprised he'd even considered she wouldn't.

"It has to be cash, ma'am."

"I may not have the exact change." Opening a wallet Walker hadn't noticed she was carrying, she began to pull out one-hundred-dollar bills. Bunches of them. "How much did you say I owe?"

Walker couldn't help but gape at her. Her wallet was crammed full of money. Where the hell had she gotten—

Pete and Lizzie proceeded with the transaction while Walker stood there dumfounded. His head was still reeling ten minutes later as he carried the last of the boxes into Susie-Q's room. The baby was sound asleep in her playpen.

He leaned the crib mattress against the wall. "Lizzie, you gotta be straight with me. Where did you get all that money?"

"Not that it's any of your concern, but I withdrew it from my own account before I left home so that I'd have cash for the trip. If you'd like, I'd be happy to pay room and board while I'm here. I should have offered earlier."

"No, that's not what I want. I just want to be damn sure that you're not—"

"Not what? A bank robber?"

He shrugged. "Something like that."

"I told you I hadn't broken the law."

"Maybe so, but you sure haven't told me the whole truth yet, have you? I think it's time."

Evading his gaze, she glanced down at the sleeping baby. "Three days before I was supposed to get married, I realized I couldn't go through with it. I didn't love him. More importantly he'd never be a loving father to Suzanne."

"You simply walked out?"

"I called my mother to let her know to cancel the ceremony."

"But not your groom?"

"No, I didn't call him. Between my mother and Vernon they might have..." She left the thought unfinished.

"Might have what? Forced you into marrying him whether you wanted to or not?"

"Yes." She brushed past Walker and stepped out into the hallway. "Vernon can be very persuasive and my mother's always been a bit domineering. I'm not...well, I'm not a very strong person."

Walker wondered if she was underestimating herself. It took a bucketful of courage to walk away from everything that was familiar and start a new life.

Drawing in a breath that raised her breasts, she looked up at him, her eyes shinning with unshed tears. "Suzanne's father was Steven Poling. We pretty much grew up together, same parties at the country club, tennis classes, similar private schools. He was the love of my life for almost as long as I can remember."

"And he died."

She nodded. "In the Amazon on a small corporate jet trying to get home to marry me after I told him I was...p-pregnant." Her voice cracked. "The plane crashed. I killed him."

Wanting to comfort her, Walker stepped forward. Her shoulders were too slender to carry that much guilt.

She held up her hand to stop him. "Mother was

devastated when she learned I was pregnant. She's all about image and social position. Appearances. For weeks after Steve died, I was in such a dark place I barely knew what was going on around me. To save face in the community, she arranged that Vernon and I announce our engagement. I didn't even care, so I went along."

"Did she think this Vernon character loved you?"

"I don't imagine the question crossed her mind. My parents have political ambitions for my brother Robert. Vernon's family is very influential, mine is wealthy."

"A marriage of convenience."

"Their convenience. Not mine or Suzanne's."

He did step forward then, closing his hands around her shoulders despite her effort to turn away. "Look at me, Lizzie."

Her chin trembled, and he wanted to take her more fully in his arms. But she'd loved and lost another man. Her grief was still too raw to accept anyone else. Likely, given her background, he wouldn't ever be that man.

"I'm glad you walked out on the wedding. You did the right thing. For both you and Susie-Q."

"I hope so." A single tear crept down her cheek.

Damn but he wanted to kiss it away. He didn't have that right.

"Please, I don't want Vernon or my family to know where I am. Not yet. Not until I decide exactly what I want to do with the rest of my life. What will be best for Suzanne. That's why I brought cash instead of using credit cards that can be traced."

It had only been four days and already he had trouble imagining a time when Susie-Q and Lizzie weren't a part of his life. He wouldn't send them away. But that didn't mean she'd stay, not for the long haul.

"As a matter of principle," she continued, "Vernon might decide to track me down. Leaving him practically standing at the altar wouldn't do much for his ego, and his ego is massive. He was probably furious when he heard I'd left town."

"You came here looking for a refuge, right?"

"Very much so. I'm sorry I wasn't totally honest with you right from the start."

"That's what the Double O has always been about, a place of refuge for those who need it."

The pleading look in her eyes touched that same soft spot Susie-Q had found when he'd held her, a deeper emotion than he'd ever felt with the boys who'd shown up on his doorstep with no place left to go. They'd come to the end of the line.

In her own way, so had Lizzie and her baby.

The phone rang, jarring him out of the moment.

Walker considered letting the answering machine pick up. Instead he decided he needed a break, some time to absorb what Lizzie had told him.

With regret, he released her. "I'd better get that."

She nodded, and he went into his bedroom to pick up the extension there.

When he returned a few minutes later, the door to Lizzie's room was open and she was silhouetted against the window, looking outside. She looked as lost as a newborn calf who had wandered away from its mother, as lost and alone as Walker still sometimes felt.

He desperately wanted to walk across the room, take her in his arms, promise her that together they wouldn't ever be lonely again.

But he couldn't do that any more than he could promise her everything would be all right. He didn't have the power to change the world. Her world and his were miles apart.

He had twenty bucks in his wallet; she had thousands.

She'd lost her one true love; he'd never found one. Maybe didn't deserve one.

Apparently sensing his presence, she said without turning around, "This is truly beautiful country. You can see all the way to the horizon."

She was beautiful, too, so much so he ached for her. But he couldn't see how they could have a future together. Somewhere out there a man was looking for her. Walker knew darn well *he'd* never stop searching for her if Lizzie had once been his to hold, arranged marriage or not.

"You'll have to plan to feed another mouth tonight," he said. "That was Mabel Cannery, a social worker from Children's Services, on the phone."

Lizzie turned. "She's coming for dinner?"

"She's bringing me another boy. A fifteen-year-old. Says he's a real piece of work. An incorrigible runaway who's had a few brushes with the law."

"I'll set another place."

"Thanks." He marveled that she'd accepted the arrival of an unexpected guest so easily. Not many women would.

"Dinner ought to be better tonight. There were two cookbooks in that delivery I got."

His lips twitched with the threat of a smile. "I'm sure the boys will be happy to hear that."

"Last night was the first time I'd ever cooked anything that wasn't already made."

"Somehow I figured as much."

Her cheeks flushed a spot of color as though kissed by the sun. "It seems like I'm forever thanking you for letting me stay. From now on, I promise I'll earn my keep."

He cleared his throat. "You're welcome here as long as you want." *Or until your groom convinces you to go back to him, whichever comes first.* "I've gotta go tell Speed we've got another boy coming. I'll come up later to put the crib together."

"I think I can manage."

He eyed the big carton skeptically. The box he'd carried upstairs was both heavy and awkward. "You'd better wait for me or one of the boys. I don't want you hurting yourself."

He left her and went downstairs. But before he went to find Speed, he made a phone call from his office.

"Hey, Sharpy, what's up?" his brother asked when he answered the phone at the sheriff's office.

"I need you to check out a Nevada license plate for me."

"You have a run in with the car?"

"Not exactly. It's on a new BMW."

Eric whistled. "You're hanging around with fancy company these days, brother."

"Just check it out and skip the comments, okay?" He gave Eric the number of Lizzie's plates. It wasn't that he didn't trust her. She'd told him the truth this time, or at least most of it. But he was cautious enough to want to avoid any trouble that would come down on the Double O. He held Oliver Oakes's legacy in his hands. He wouldn't do anything, even for a beautiful woman, that would put the ranch at risk.

"I'll check the plates, but it'll mean you owe me a favor."

Walker stifled a groan. "Like what?"

"I don't know yet." Walker could hear the grin in Eric's voice. "But I'll think of something."

Troubled, Walker hung up the phone. From the living room he heard the vacuum. Apparently his housekeeper was taking her job to heart.

Almost immediately there was a popping sound and Lizzie screamed.

"What the heck?" He shoved back from his desk, anxious to find out what was wrong.

What he found was a woman covered from head to toe with dust. Her hair was gray with it and so was her dress. And she was sobbing, muddy tears already streaking her face.

"What happened?"

She shook an accusing finger at the upright vacuum standing in the middle of the living-room rug where it was surrounded by a mountain of the same dust that covered her. "It blew up! That damn thing was booby-trapped!" she cried hysterically.

"Yeah, I can see that." He stifled a smile. "Looks like the bag was overfull. Whoever used it last should have changed it."

"Bag? What bag?"

"This." He showed her the tattered remains of the disposable bag. "There ought to be some replacements in the closet where the vacuum is stored."

"My God, why didn't anyone ever tell me these damn things had *bags* inside?" She threw up her hands in dismay and choked on another sob. "Do you know I can speak three different languages? *Fluently.* I can tell at a glance what artist painted every damn picture in the Louvre and discuss their various styles. *At length,* damn it! Why in hell didn't anyone teach me a damn thing that was useful?"

She totally broke down then, and Walker wrapped his arms around her. Damn, she felt good. Slender. Her small breasts pressing against his chest. Her hips nestled just so against his pelvis.

"Shh, Lizzie, honey. You don't have to know stuff like this. It's okay."

"No, it's not." She hiccuped. "I wanted the house to look nice for the social worker. I didn't want her to think...to think that you live in a pigsty."

"It's all right. We'll get the mess cleaned up." Risking his own self-control, he brushed a kiss to her temple. Not even a bag full of dust could mask her sweet sultry scent or make her any less sexy.

"I'm...sorry."

He wasn't. It might take a while to clean up the mess but it was a sacrifice he'd be willing to make any day of the week in exchange for an excuse to hold Lizzie in his arms.

COCKY DID NOT BEGIN TO describe Frankie Morisi. Short for his age and skinny, he strutted like a rooster in a henhouse. Elizabeth didn't need a degree in psychology to know it was all show. The youngster was scared to death.

"Hey, I ain't gonna stay here any longer than the last place. I'll fill up on some grub and then I'm outta here." He reached across the table for a platter of home-fried potatoes and onions.

Fridge's hand came down on his arm—hard. "Miss Lizzie gets to serve herself first."

"Ah, come on. I ain't waiting on any bi—"

In a move so quick, Elizabeth barely saw it, Fridge twisted the new boy's arm behind his back. "We *all* wait, got it?"

Walker jerked his head at the pair. "Fridge is right, Chicago. Lizzie will serve herself and then we all pass the bowls and platters around. That's called manners. Let him go, Fridge."

As quickly as she could, Elizabeth served herself a few slices of potatoes. They were too greasy for her liking but the calories wouldn't hurt the boys. She passed the plate to Frankie.

Grudgingly he took it. "How long you been shacked up with him?" In a gesture much like Walker's, he jerked his head toward the opposite end of the table. "I could show you a good time, if you're tired of hanging out with an old guy like him."

Elizabeth reached for the plate of hamburger patties, as much to hide her smile as anything else. "We've got mustard, mayonnaise, pickle relish, sliced tomatoes and onions. I didn't know what you'd all like."

"I'd like of piece of—"

Frankie found himself pulled up from his chair by the back of his shirt. Walker marched him out of the room quick step. Elizabeth winced. That young man was about to get the lecture of his life. And he deserved it.

"Now, then," she said, smiling at Speed and the boys, "do you think I ought to feed Frankie some of my special two-bean salad to sweeten him up? Or should we let him back to the table to have hamburgers with the rest of us when Walker is done with him?"

Everyone broke up in laughter over her comment. She felt an enormous sense of accomplishment. In some strange way, she'd been accepted by these young men. Not because she was a woman. Or even because she was pretty. But because she was *one* of them. More so than they realized. She, too, was a runaway in search of a refuge.

A few minutes later, Walker and a chastened Frankie returned to the table with no visible wounds in either case. The boy sullenly accepted the plate of hamburgers Elizabeth passed him.

"Tomorrow we have to move the herd in the lower pasture to the north pasture," Walker said.

"Isn't it a little early for that, boss?" Speed asked.

"Nope. I rode out there yesterday. There's so little grass in the lower pasture, the cows will be eating sticks and rocks pretty soon. I need 'em closer to the river where there's more moisture." He squeezed enough catsup on his burger to count as his serving of vegetables for the day. "With this drought, I'm afraid of overgrazing the pastures. If we do that, the grass won't come back next year."

"Gotcha, boss." Having made quick work of the first, Speed reached for a second hamburger. "Supper's real good, ma'am."

Elizabeth smiled her thanks.

"Can I ride lead this time?" Fridge asked. "I was eatin' dust at drag last time we moved a herd."

Walker glanced around the table. "Hearing no objections, you're it. Chicago, you know how to ride?"

"Yeah, I used to ride the El all the time," the boy muttered in reference to the elevated commuter train that ran through Chicago.

"Ride a horse," Walker clarified with barely concealed impatience.

"Hell—heck no. Where would I learn a dumb thing like that?"

"Sounds like tomorrow morning is a good time to start."

"Naw, I'll just hang out around here."

Walker ignored the boy's comment. "Bean Pole, I'd like you to show Chicago the ropes, how to saddle a horse, you know the drill. Let's try him on Devil Wind first."

Chicago's head snapped up. "Devil Wind?"

Scotty snickered under his breath. "Gotta watch out for Devil Wind. He'll knock you right out of the saddle."

Chicago gave the younger boy a dirty look. "Then I'll knock you right—"

"I'd like to go along, too, if I may," Elizabeth said, interrupting the argument. "I'd like to see the rest of the ranch."

"I think it would be better if I drove you around in the truck another time. You've got the baby and all to worry about."

"We'll be fine," she assured him, smiling sweetly. It had been a couple of years since she'd been on a horse but riding wasn't something you forgot. And she'd been damn good at it as a teenager, with a nice collection of blue ribbons to show for her efforts.

In retrospect, she thought grimly, her time might have been better spent learning to operate a vacuum cleaner.

WALKER TAPPED HIS HEELS to his horse's flanks and lightly reined him away from the herd to coax a wayward yearling back into line. Not that Magic needed much direction. The quarter horse gelding knew more about moving cows than he did, often anticipating what a cow would do before the cow knew it herself. On a big roundup, Magic was easily worth two hired hands for all the work he saved Walker and his cowboys.

The boys were spaced out around the forty head

they were moving, Fridge on the left shoulder of the lead animal, right where he should be. Bean Pole and Chicago were riding together, the new boy with a death grip on the saddle horn. Dust billowed beneath the herd and drifted back toward Speed and Scotty, who were riding drag. Right behind them came Bandit, a black-and-white flash that went after a wayward heifer almost before a rider could recognize the cow had wandered.

Glancing over his shoulder, Walker spotted another horse cantering across the rolling grassland toward them, the rider spending more time out of the saddle than in it.

Squinting, he tipped his hat back and frowned. What the hell did Lizzie think she was doing? He thought she'd given up on the idea of coming with them. And what had she done with Susie-Q? Surely she hadn't left the baby at the house alone.

He reined Magic around to meet her before she spooked the herd and pulled up in front of her. To his amazement she had Susie-Q in the soft carrier snuggled against her chest.

"You're going to jiggle that baby to death riding like that," he said.

"Nonsense. I don't jiggle. I *post*, although that isn't easy in a Western saddle. I couldn't find a proper one."

"A proper—" He sputtered in astonishment. "You're posting English style on an Appaloosa? God, if anybody finds out, I'm going to be the biggest laughingstock in Montana."

She tossed her pretty little chin up in the air. "It's how I learned to ride. And I'll have you know, Suzanne is loving it."

Admittedly the baby did appear content in her carrier but that didn't mean Lizzie should have brought her along. "A roundup, even a small one like this, is dirty, dusty work. Not a fit place for a baby."

"She'll be fine. I'll stay off to the side out of harm's way."

Walker wasn't convinced. "The horse you're riding doesn't have the best disposition in the world. I usually save Tillamook for an experienced cowhand."

"He and I are getting along just fine. Aren't we, boy?" The horse's ears swiveled back as she spoke to him and patted his sweaty neck. "Shouldn't we be catching up with the herd?"

This was one argument Walker sensed he would lose. He had to give her credit for stubbornness. He could only hope she knew what she was doing and wouldn't hurt herself or the baby.

"All right. But try to keep your pretty little rear end in the saddle or we'll have the cows rolling over laughing so hard they won't be able to get up and walk."

She made a derisive noise but her eyes twinkled, and she smiled. "Someday I'll show you my riding trophies, Mr. Sharp Shooter. Then we'll see what you have to say about where my rear end belongs."

"Be careful what you ask for, Slick. You might get more than you bargained for." He wheeled Magic around, trotting toward the herd. He knew exactly where he'd like Lizzie's rear end to be—in the palm of his hands as he entered her.

And that kind of thinking would get them both into more trouble than either of them could handle.

Elizabeth caught up with Walker, drawing her horse into step beside his. She'd been taken aback by his comment as well as the matching thrill of excitement that had coursed through her body. In his hooded eyes, she'd seen a vision of them together, intimately entwined, and the startling clarity of that picture had taken her breath away.

She had no right to dream of a relationship with Walker. Or even to want one. She'd imposed on his hospitality, lied to him and pleaded with him to give her refuge. He'd already gone beyond what most men would have done. To take further advantage of the friendship he'd offered when her own life was still in disarray would be the height of unfairness to them both.

She'd made enough mistakes in her life already. For Suzanne's sake, she couldn't add foolhardiness to her list of weaknesses.

Which didn't mean she couldn't admire his seat in a saddle, the way he moved as though part of his mount, the man and animal of the same mind as they walked beside the herd. His blue chambray shirt pulled tautly across his shoulders, flexing slightly with each motion of the horse. His thighs were rock-hard, covered by leather chaps, his rear end neat and gloved by faded jeans. A man of the land comfortable with himself.

Yes, she could admire but she didn't dare touch. Because she was confident, once she touched Walker in an intimate way and he touched her in return, she'd never be satisfied with anything less.

And that would be a betrayal of her love for Steve.

The farther from the main ranch house they rode, the more wild the countryside became. Hidden in the grass were clusters of wildflowers, tiny pale blue and white petals waving in a light breeze. Meadowlarks skirted across the landscape diving for bugs stirred up by the passing herd. The air was filled with the scents of elemental life, sage and grass, cows and horses, and the linseed oil rubbed into the soft leather of her saddle.

"The new boy seems to be getting along all right on his horse," she commented into the silence broken only by an occasional cow mooing or the soft calls of one youngster to another. "I can't think why you named that horse Devil Wind. He looks placid enough to me."

"He's our gentlest mount, the one I start all the boys on."

"Then why—"

"He's got a funny digestion problem. You don't want to be downwind from Devil Wind right after he eats his bag of oats."

She puzzled over his answer until it registered just what Walker was talking about. "Oh, good heavens!" She laughed. "That is such a guy thing to name a horse because of that."

He grinned at her. "Welcome to Montana, where

men are men and make jokes about bodily functions whenever they get the chance.''

With a shake of her head, she rode on. Not that the men in her social circle didn't make jokes like that. They just didn't let her in on the secret.

Apparently gaining more confidence on his horse, Chicago yelled, ''Can't these stupid cows go any faster? I thought you hicks were real cowboys.''

''Easy, son. Cows don't like to be rushed,'' Walker called to him.

The youngster gave him a scathing look. ''I ain't your son or anybody else's.'' He took off his hat, waved it in the air and shouted, ''Come on, you lazy no goods! Get movin'!'' He kicked his horse right into the center of the herd.

Bandit barked a warning and raced after a yearling that had been spooked.

The cows started and bawled. One bucked with its back feet, striking another. The others jockeyed to get away, which startled the rest of the yearlings into flight. The mother cows panicked and went after their babies.

Walker swore under his breath and his horse took off after one of the frightened animals.

Elizabeth saw another cow escape the herd. She nudged her horse into pursuit. With barely a command from her, Tillamook proceeded to run down the animal, wheeling the cow around until she was headed back toward the herd.

Everything was going fine, and Elizabeth was beginning to congratulate herself for being such a good cowboy, when the cow dropped out of sight in a gully five feet deep and half again as wide.

Using one hand to brace Suzanne against her chest, Elizabeth stood in her stirrups, signaling Tillamook to bridge the distance in one leap, the effort no more difficult than the obstacles she'd faced a hundred times in three-day eventing competitions.

Chapter Seven

Walker saw Lizzie's horse leave the ground. Panic rocketed through him and his heart snagged in his throat. In that instant he wanted to kill Chicago with his bare hands for starting the damn stampede.

When Lizzie landed safely on the far side of the dry wash, horse and rider expertly turning the wayward cow back into the herd, he exhaled in relief. But that didn't get Chicago off the hook—or Lizzie—for doing such a damn fool thing.

No thanks to Chicago, they got the cows calmed down and back in line. Walker was particularly proud of Fridge, who turned the lead cow in a circle, bunching them all together again. The boy beamed at the praise Walker gave him. The youngster had come a long way in the two years since he arrived at the Double O.

At this point, Walker wasn't sure Frankie Morisi would last two days. The boy's cocky grin wasn't one that asked for forgiveness.

"Here's your next lesson, Chicago. You're gonna ride drag the rest of the way, and when we get back to the ranch, you'll muck the horse stalls. All of them.''

''Muck? I ain't gonna do—''

''And if you ever pull a stunt like that again, you'll be on your hands and knees scrubbing the stalls with your own toothbrush. You got that?''

The boy muttered a vile word under his breath. Since Walker hadn't heard it clearly, he let it go. This time.

''Scotty, change places with Chicago. He's riding drag now.''

''Right, boss!'' With a grin, the youngster trotted up beside Bean Pole.

Lizzie was the next person on his list. He wheeled his horse in her direction. She looked as happy as a turkey the day after Thanksgiving. His heart was still doing jumping jacks in his chest.

''What in the name of heaven were you doing back there?''

''Herding cattle. Wasn't that great? I haven't had that much fun in ages.''

He glared at her. She didn't seem to notice. ''You could have been killed jumping that dry wash. Susie-Q, too.''

''Nonsense. It wasn't very wide.'' She patted her horse's neck. ''Tillamook responded beautifully, didn't you, boy? Right in stride.''

She was the most irritating woman! He'd been scared out of his head for her, and she acted as though it was the most normal thing in the world for a woman and baby to go leaping across a six-foot-deep gully. She could have broken her fool neck!

"How many years have you been riding?" he asked, his fears colliding with his irritation.

"I was on a horse before I could walk. I entered my first show when I was six."

"Jumping?"

"Very low rails," she conceded.

Great. She'd been riding longer than he had and at fancy equestrian events, from the sounds of it. In her world, she'd ridden for fun and pleasure. In his, mounting a horse was all in a day's work.

The man she'd given her heart to had been part of that same wealthy country-club set.

How could Walker compete with that?

Telling himself that life wasn't about competition, he rode off. Lizzie wasn't a trophy meant for a man to win.

But even as the thought came to him, he knew it was a lie. He *wanted* her. But he knew what the answer would be.

As a twelve-year-old kid he'd wanted a lot of things—a ten-speed bike, a skateboard with fancy wheels, a mother who hadn't dumped him at the grocery store.

Somehow he hadn't been good enough to deserve any of that. Hard to imagine things had changed much in the past twenty years.

But a part of him wanted to find out.

WALKER RELEASED THE COWS to graze and the boys to cool off in the shallow river nearby. Elizabeth suspected the youngsters would be skinny-dipping if she weren't around. Out of deference to her, they'd kept on their shorts.

She smiled, regretting that Walker, at least, hadn't elected to skinny-dip anyway. His powerful body would be a sight to behold. But devoted cowboy that he was, he was spending his time seeing to the horses downstream, letting the animals quench their thirst.

Knowing Suzanne was getting hungry, Elizabeth found a shady spot under a cottonwood tree and spread out the blanket she'd brought along in her saddlebags. Around a bend away from where the boys were playing, she settled down with her back resting against the tree to give the baby her bottle.

With the air warm and the sound of insects humming in counterpoint to the distant laughter of the boys, she closed her eyes, drifting on the pleasant aftermath that comes with physical exertion.

Dreamlike, she felt his lips on hers. She knew the shape of them, their fullness and warmth as though he had kissed her a thousand times before. He played his mouth over hers with the skill of an expert, a slow meeting and mating, a deliberate exploration. Tantalizing her. Drawing from her a moan that came from deep in her throat.

She opened her eyes, unsurprised to find Walker was no dream but a flesh and blood man. He'd removed his Stetson, leaving a damp imprint on his saddle-brown hair. His dilated pupils were as dark as a midnight sky, and a teasing smile curled his lips.

"I couldn't resist waking Sleeping Beauty. I hope you don't mind."

She *should* mind. His was a dangerous game with much at stake for them both. But she couldn't bring herself to say the words that would send him away. Not when she could feel his seductive heat so close to her. Not when that same warmth was circling through her body, forcing her to ignore the memories of the past, demanding she ask for more in the present.

She glanced around, noting that the boys were still out of sight. "No, I don't mind."

His strong hand, callused by the work of a cowboy, slid around to cup the back of her neck, and he dipped his head toward hers again. This time his mouth was more insistent, his tongue sliding along the seam of her lips while his fingers at her neck slipped through the hair at her nape, releasing the twist tucked up under her hat.

His fingers kneaded her scalp while he kept on kissing her, making her pulse quicken at the same time she lost all sense of reason. She gave herself over to the taste of him, his sweet masculine flavor, the baby between them assuring that things couldn't go too far too fast.

With an audible groan, he sat back on his haunches and removed her hat. Her hair fell to her shoulders. "I've wanted to see your hair down since the day you showed up at the Double O."

"All you needed to do was ask." Her throat was tight, her voice husky.

"I'll keep that in mind the next time I get the urge."

She had urges, too, ones Elizabeth knew she had to keep in check. But dear heaven, it would be so easy to give in to them. To lay the baby down on the blanket and draw Walker to her, beg him to ease the ache that still had her trembling for him. Do it right here on a grassy knoll beneath a cottonwood tree with four adolescent boys and the ranch foreman barely out of sight.

He glanced down at her hands. "What happened to your fingernails?"

Holding up her hands, she waggled her fingers, the nails shorter than she'd worn them in years and coated with only clear polish. "I broke a nail yesterday. I didn't exactly spot a manicurist shop in town, so I thought it would be better to trim them to a more manageable length."

Taking her hands, he brought both of them to his lips, kissing them and sending shivers down her spine.

"I liked them long," he whispered, his voice husky. "Ranching is hard on a woman's hands."

Hard on her heart, too, from the feel of her thundering pulse.

The baby moved and whimpered.

"Ah, the second Sleeping Beauty." Releasing her hands, Walker leaned over and cupped the top of Suzanne's head, brushing a kiss to her cheek. "We'll have to be heading back now."

Elizabeth nodded. "Yes, that would be the wise thing to do."

"Damn hard being smart all the time, isn't it?"

More difficult than Elizabeth had ever imagined.

THE NEXT FEW DAYS WENT smoothly, assuming Elizabeth could ignore the electricity in the air whenever she and Walker were in the same room. Her body hummed with it as if a summer electrical storm were right overhead, a lightning bolt about to strike.

And on the inside, her guilty conscience waged a continuous battle not to allow her memories of Steve—and her love for him—to fade. But Walker was here. Alive. Potently masculine.

Steve was gone. With each passing day, details of their time together slipped away to be replaced by the image of Walker striding toward her from the corral or the quick flash of his smile across the table.

She spent her time caring for Suzanne and improving her culinary skills. She read through her cookbooks, the boys suggesting their favorite meals. In an effort to break through Frankie's sullen facade, she'd even driven into town earlier in the day to buy the ingredients for his favorite Mulligan stew. And then she burned it so badly, she threw out the pot and made them all ham sandwiches.

No one made progress without an occasional backward step, she told herself as she drifted off to sleep that evening. Suzanne had been restless all day, which is why she'd lost track of stirring the pot. She'd do better next time.

A while later, Suzanne's cries woke her. According to the clock by her bed it was still two hours until dawn.

Elizabeth groaned as she struggled up and pulled on her robe. Suzanne hadn't eaten well the previous day and now she was probably hungry. The baby's cries quieted when Elizabeth picked her up.

"If you'd taken all your bottle before bedtime, we both could have slept later, sweetie."

Yawning, she carried the baby downstairs and into the kitchen, where she mixed a bottle of formula. Maybe Suzanne would go back to bed after this and she'd still get another hour of sleep herself.

She'd just started to give the bottle to Suzanne when she heard a noise coming from Walker's office. Curious, she went to investigate.

It wasn't Walker sitting at his desk but Frankie, going through the drawers.

"What are you up to, Chicago?"

He jumped at the sound of her voice. "Jeez, you scared me to death."

"You would have been more than scared if it had been Walker who walked in on you."

"He's a tyrant, always ordering me around and stuff. I ain't gonna stay here no more."

Calmly she settled on the leather chair in the corner of the room, offering Suzanne her bottle. "And that's why you were going through Walker's personal things?"

"I'm lookin' for money, that's what. He's got to have some cash here somewhere."

"Just where were you planning to go?"

"It don't matter. Just away from here."

"How many places have you run away from, Frankie? Five? Ten?"

He answered with a sullen lift of his shoulders.

"Then maybe this is the end of the line. Maybe the

Double O is the last, best chance for you to turn your life around."

"Why the hell would I want to?"

"Because you're scared. Just like I was when I came here. Just like Scotty and Bean Pole and Fridge were. Walker, too, for that matter."

He eyed her skeptically but his look of belligerence was gone. "What are you talking about?"

She told him she was running, too, although she didn't give him the details. And shared with him what she knew of the boys as well as Walker.

"Walker and the Double O will give you a chance to figure out who you want to be," she concluded. "But you have to give them a chance, too."

His shoulders slumped. "I probably couldn't hitch a ride on the road this early in the morning anyway," he mumbled.

"Probably not." She nearly punched her fist in the air. For the moment, she'd won. She'd gained a little more time for Frankie to come to terms with himself and his own past. Working with a runaway, she knew instinctively that was a major victory.

Suzanne had fallen asleep in her arms. Elizabeth lifted the baby to her shoulder. "I've got to put Susie-Q back down. With luck, she'll sleep a couple more hours." She glanced at the clock, which read almost five. "Why don't you slip back into the bunkhouse and catch a few more *z*'s yourself?"

"I guess." He did his shoulder lift but with far less arrogance now. "See you later, okay?"

"I'll be here." For a while, at least. Like Frankie, she couldn't predict how long. The time would come when she'd have to face her own past—Vernon and her parents. Her brother, too, whose future political career she could well have hampered when she'd bolted. She'd like to put all of those confrontations off as long as possible.

She carried her sleeping baby upstairs and laid her down in the crib. The little minx was sleeping like an angel while she was wiped out from being awakened at three in the morning.

As she left Suzanne's room, she nearly collided with Walker.

"What are you doing up at this hour?" he asked. He'd shaved already and was fully dressed, leaving her at the disadvantage of still being in her robe and nightgown. His appreciative gaze swept over her, bringing a flush to her flesh.

"Besides dealing with Susie-Q, who has gotten herself off schedule, I've been playing counselor for one of your adolescents."

He lifted his brows, and she told him what had happened downstairs with Frankie.

"Sounds like you did good with the boy, Slick."

"I don't know how long our chat will last," she admitted. "But it will probably give the boy a few more days to adjust to being here. Guess that's all we can expect with a youngster that troubled."

"I noticed right from the start that you seem to know how to deal with these kids. It's a real talent."

She flushed with his approval. "You know, when I

started college, I wanted to be a social worker. My parents nixed the idea.''

"Too down and dirty for them?''

"Probably. They thought I'd do better if I studied art and music, liberal arts classes. I'd become a better conversationalist, they assured me. But I still managed to take a bunch of psychology courses.''

"Right now, I think Chicago ought to be grateful you took some of those psych classes. They might just save his bacon.''

"I hope so.''

To her surprise, he dipped his head and brushed a quick kiss to her lips. "Get some sleep. We'll manage for breakfast on our own.''

Sleep? Right!

Even that swift brush of his lips was likely to keep her body tingling with wanting for the next several hours.

Damn it all! It wasn't fair she should want a man so much and couldn't—*shouldn't*—have him.

IN THE KITCHEN, WALKER measured coffee for the pot and poured in the water.

It figured Lizzie had a college degree. When she spoke, her bluesy voice sounded both classy and educated. She likely knew everything there was to know about art and music.

In contrast, Walker knew nothing at all about art except what he'd picked up as an adolescent from girlie magazines. What he knew about music was pretty much limited to whatever tune he happened to hear on the radio, and he could never tell one musician from another.

What he *did* know were cows—breeding and raising, buying and selling, and every known disease that could affect the animals. He'd learned on the job and from the books crammed onto the shelves in his office. Still, cows and their mating habits weren't likely to be typical topics of conversation at the country clubs where Lizzie had spent her time.

Watching the coffee drip into the pot, he chided himself for liking her kisses too much and for wanting more.

A cowboy and a city slicker weren't a likely combination.

FRIDAY NIGHTS MEANT ice-cream cones at Harold Hudson's Drugstore, or so Walker informed Elizabeth after dinner.

"There's not much entertainment for teenagers around here so the kids hang out at the drugstore on Friday nights and cruise Main Street," he told her. "It gives the boys a chance to ogle the girls."

"And vice versus," she commented, eyeing a gaggle of adolescent girls in front of the store dressed uniformly in jeans and tank tops. Each one held a cone in her hand, making it a point not to notice the arrival of the boys from the Double O.

Elizabeth suppressed a smile and adjusted Suzanne in her carrier. How well she remembered the dances at her all-girls boarding school. When the boys arrived from a neighboring school, not a one of the girls would even look in their direction, and the boys weren't any more eager to mix it up. Only the head teacher's insistence forced the sexes together, or so they all told each other later, giggling over who had danced with whom and how many times.

Remaining faithful to Steve—who attended school thousands of miles away—Elizabeth had never been the belle of the ball.

With the warmth of Walker's hand at the small of her back, she entered the store. The shelves were cluttered with everything from comic books to shampoo and cough syrup; the pharmacy was in the back. The pharmacist, who looked to be as old as Grass Valley itself, was up front dispensing ice-cream cones from a glass-fronted freezer.

Fridge, Bean Pole and Scotty made a beeline for the ice cream. Frankie sauntered in more nonchalantly, giving the girls a good chance to look him over.

"What'll you have, youngsters?" Harold asked, peering over the top of his reading glasses.

"Double chocolate and strawberry," Fridge announced.

Harold shook his head. "Single scoop for you, young man. One or the other, not both."

"Ah, come on. You only let me have one scoop last time."

"Same as this time." Bending, he dipped into the five-gallon bucket of chocolate and loaded up a cone, passing it to Fridge. "Who's next?"

Bean Pole and Scotty got double scoops of chocolate mint without argument but when it was Frankie's turn, the white-jacketed pharmacist refused the boy's order of double scoops of praline and French vanilla. "You look like lemon to me."

"Lemon! No way, man! I want—"

"Better take what he'll give you, Chicago," Walker said. "Harold's got a way of making up his own mind what he serves to his customers."

Frankie sputtered, accepting the bright yellow two-scoop cone with a frown.

"You learn how to smile, young man, or you'll always be puckered up like that."

With a certain amount of trepidation, Elizabeth gazed into the display case trying to make a decision. It wasn't hard. "I'll have a single Rocky Road cone, please."

"Nope. No chocolate for you. It'll go right through your milk and give that sweet little baby colic, sure as shootin'."

"Go right through—" She shook her head, realizing what he meant. "No, I'm not nursing."

"You should be, but it still don't matter. Vanilla's best anyway."

"But I—"

He handed her a cone with an extra-large scoop of French vanilla on top and winked. "You and young Walker will both sleep better tonight this way."

Next to her, Elizabeth heard Walker make a choked sound as though swallowing a laugh. "Instead of ordering, why don't you tell me what I am going to have tonight?"

"Fun." Grinning, Harold scooped up peaches-and-cream and piled it on a cone.

Nearly choking herself, Elizabeth fled the store, Walker following when he'd paid for the ice cream. Only when she reached his truck, which he'd parked across the street, did she allow herself to laugh out loud. "I don't believe that man."

Walker helped her into the truck cab. "One of Grass Valley's more colorful characters."

"Has he always been like that? Telling people what they're supposed to eat?"

"As long as I can remember." He closed her door and went around to the driver's side. "I'll trade you if you don't like vanilla."

"Actually it's delicious. I just usually order chocolate."

"Well, then…" He settled behind the steering wheel and licked his cone. "Maybe ol' Harold knew what he was doing."

Maybe so, but only when it came to ice cream. His suggestive comments about *sleeping* and *fun* were off the mark. She slept alone. So did Walker.

She sighed. That wasn't nearly as much fun as Harold might imagine.

ELIZABETH SPENT THE BETTER part of Saturday night boiling and peeling potatoes for a salad for the Sunday potluck at church. She chopped onions until her eyes flooded with tears, diced hard-boiled eggs, added as much pickle relish as they had on hand and prayed the mayonnaise wouldn't give anyone food poisoning if it sat out too long.

Hetty Moore, the owner of the general store, was the first one to corral her after the service was over. Her Sunday-best dress looked like it might have been in style in the forties, with a tiny floral print and huge shoulder pads. "Let's put that bowl of potato salad on this table with the others," she said.

Hetty took the bowl, which left Elizabeth's hands free to soothe Suzanne, who'd been fussy during most of the church service.

"Oh, dear, it looks like everyone had the same idea today," Elizabeth said when she reached the tables set up for the potluck. One whole table was covered with dishes filled with every possible variation of potato salad. "I wish someone had suggested I bring something else. With so many varieties, no one will want mine."

"Not at all, dear. Everyone will be anxious to try yours."

"It's just plain old-fashioned potato salad." Directly from her *Cooking, Quick and Easy* cookbook.

"I'll tell you a little secret, dear." Peering over the top of her half-glasses, Hetty glanced around to be sure no one was listening. "Marlene Huhn makes the most dreadful German salad. Way too much vinegar. And Abby Treadwell never cooks her potatoes enough. It's like eating them raw. Valery Haywood adds whatever leftovers she has around the house. One time, I swear she added little bite-size doggie biscuits. By comparison, I'm sure yours will be delicious."

Elizabeth choked back a laugh. "Do they always bring the same thing to the potluck?"

"Pretty much. I've asked the preacher to have a talk with them, but he says it's the Lord's way to accept what they bring with a smile."

"That's very generous of him." She could only hope the preacher would be just as kind if her contribution gave him a bad case of indigestion.

Suzanne started fussing again. The only time she'd been quiet all morning was when she'd been taking her bottle, giving the preacher some blessed quiet in which to deliver his sermon. But the silence hadn't lasted long.

"Here, let me take that sweet baby a minute," Hetty said.

"I don't know what's been wrong with her lately." She'd been up with the baby again last night. At three and a half months, Suzanne should be sleeping through the night, or so she'd hoped.

"Raised six of these precious bundles myself. If anyone can quiet her, I can."

Lifting Suzanne from her Snugli carrier, Elizabeth handed Hettie the baby. Despite the woman's best efforts, the crying persisted. Within minutes, the pathetic sobs acted as a magnet, drawing half the women in the congregation to see what was going on.

Valery Haywood suggested the problem was colic and kindly offered a surefire cure. Marlene Huhn, her German accent thick, insisted Hetty check to see no diaper pin was sticking the poor baby, despite Elizabeth's assurances she was using pinless disposable diapers. And Abby Treadwell was confident the baby had developed an allergy to her formula, which is what had happened to her third son.

By now Suzanne was sobbing and waving her little arms around. Elizabeth tried to get her baby back from Hetty, but the discussion of Suzanne's distress was so animated, no one paid a bit of attention to her.

Dr. Justine pushed her way through the circle of well-meaning women. "Can't a one of you ladies recognize an infant with an ear infection? Here, give me that baby."

"Ear infection?" Elizabeth gasped.

"Fever, too, by the feel of her." Despite the doctor's gruff mannerisms, Suzanne quieted, resting her head on the woman's bony shoulder. "You come with me over to my office now. I'll give her a shot."

A shot? My God, her baby was ill and Elizabeth hadn't even known it. What kind of an awful mother was she?

"You listen to Dr. Justine, dear," Hetty said. "She's taken care of every baby in the county for the past fifty years and knows what to do."

She was supposed to turn her baby over to a country doctor with who knew what kind of credentials? Elizabeth had always seen specialists when she needed medical treatment. How could she—

"Come on, honey," the doctor said. "Let's get this little lady looked at." With that, Dr. Justine went striding away with Suzanne in her arms.

"Wait!" Frantically Elizabeth looked around. "I have to tell Walker. I can't just leave—"

"I'll let your man know where you've gone." Valery patted her kindly on her arm. "I know Walker will be just as worried about his little baby girl as you are."

"No, Suzanne isn't—"

"Run along now," Abby encouraged her. "We'll take care of everything here."

Elizabeth didn't have much choice. The doctor was already halfway across the parking lot, and Elizabeth couldn't see Walker anywhere.

Panic welled up in her. She broke into a run to follow the doctor. She didn't want to lose sight of her baby.

WALKER HAD BEEN TALKING with some of the other ranchers in the neighborhood when Eric pulled him aside, ushering him around the corner of the church away from the crowd. His expression was serious.

"Sorry it took me so long to get back to you about the license plate," he said.

"You found out something?" Walker had intentionally not followed up on his request to Eric. Sometimes you asked questions you really didn't want to hear the answer to. When Eric hadn't gotten right back to him, Walker had been afraid this might be one of those times. Besides, Lizzie had pretty well told him what he'd wanted to know.

"Something, but it doesn't make a whole lot of sense."

Walker's Sunday-morning good spirits took a nose-dive. He didn't like the sound of that. "Tell me."

"The plate's registered to a Buck Pettigrew, or at least it was."

"Was?"

"Mr. Pettigrew drove a four-wheel-drive Jeep that he totaled about six months ago going off the highway from Sparks to Reno. He ended up in a Reno hospital and the car went directly to a junkyard. He was trying to make an insurance claim when the switch was discovered."

Trying to make sense of what he'd just heard, Walker stared at his brother. "Somebody switched the plates?"

"I'd say that was probably the case."

"Why?"

Eric shrugged. "There could be several reasons."

"Do you think she stole the BMW?" Lizzie had said she hadn't broken the law. He wanted to believe her. But maybe she actually knew this Pettigrew person. Maybe he was the influential man she was running from. Lizzie hadn't actually said where her home was. It could be Reno, he supposed. Or somewhere else.

"There's no way of knowing unless I run the car registration and VIN number. Even then, it might be that someone sold her a stolen car without her knowing it."

Walker jammed his fingers into his hip pockets and gazed off toward the mountains and the cloudless sky. The story she'd told him about Steve and this Vernon character she'd been urged to marry had seemed so real. Sincere. But over the years more than one runaway had lied to him. He just didn't want Lizzie to do that to him, too. "I'll ask her."

"Don't get yourself in over your head with this woman until you know the facts, Sharpy. You could end up shooting yourself in the foot again."

"Yeah, I know." And his brother's warning had probably come too late.

Slowly they walked back to the front of the church to join the others, only to be met by Hetty Moore. She hurried toward them as fast as her weight and arthritic knees allowed.

"Oh, I'm so glad I found you!" she cried.

"What's wrong?" Walker asked, frowning. He glanced around in search of Lizzie.

"That dear girl of yours—Lizzie, isn't it?"

His attention snapped back to Hetty. "What happened to her?"

"Not her. The baby."

"Susie-Q?" Like wildfire, fear rose up in him uninvited. "What's wrong? Where is she?"

"Now, now. Don't get yourself all in a dither. Dr. Justine has everything under control."

"The doctor—"

"They've all gone over to Justine's office. She's going to give that sweet little baby a shot. I'm sure it's nothing—"

Walker didn't wait for the rest of Hetty's story. He was off like a rodeo rider coming out of the shoot. Eric and Speed would watch out for the boys.

A knot twisted in his belly as he ran through the parking lot and across the street to the doctor's office.

He had to see for himself what was wrong with Susie-Q. He prayed it wasn't anything serious.

Susie-Q wasn't even his own child, and he was worried sick as he burst into the doctor's office. How in hell did any father survive so much as a baby's sniffles without losing his mind?

Chapter Eight

"I feel so guilty."

Lizzie had been hovering over Susie-Q's crib since they got back from town. The doctor had given the baby an antibiotic and some medicine for the fever, and now the infant was sleeping peacefully. But you wouldn't have known that from the miserable look on Lizzie's face.

Walker was at a loss to know how to help her. And, if the truth be known, he had been as worried about Susie-Q as Lizzie. Fortunately the doctor had assured them both the baby would be fine.

"You've got to stop beating yourself up," Walker said. "All babies get sick."

"But I didn't even realize there was something wrong. I thought she was just being fussy. What kind of a mother does that make me?"

"So you're not a genius when it comes to parenting. No first-time mother is."

She snorted. "I certainly fit somewhere in the be-low-average category."

He slid his arm around her slender waist. "Come

on, you need to eat something. I'll make you a sand-wich." They had skipped the potluck, opting to bring Susie-Q back to the ranch instead. Neither one of them would have been able to eat anyway.

"No. I'm not hungry. You go ahead." She glanced up at him, her blue eyes watery. "I don't want to leave her."

If Lizzie wouldn't go to the mountain, then he'd bring the mountain to her. "I'll be back in a minute. Don't go away."

It took him more than a minute to fix sandwiches and pour glasses of milk, but when he returned she was standing right where he'd left her. He placed the tray on the changing table and went across the hall for a straight-back chair, which he brought into the nurs-ery.

"Here you go. Sit down before you collapse."

"I'm fine, really." Despite the exhaustion apparent in the lines of strain around her eyes, she shook her head.

"All right, I've got a better idea." Sitting down himself, he closed his hands around her waist and pulled her onto his lap. "Now we can both watch her."

Instead of fighting him, she drew a shaky sob and rested her head on his shoulder. She didn't weigh much at all, less than a bale of hay and her soft curves converged with his chest and thighs. He folded his arms around her, inhaling the sweet scent of violets in her hair.

"I'm afraid to take my eyes off of her for fear she'll stop breathing," she whispered.

"That's probably an overreaction," he said calmly, although he could understand her feelings. He found watching Susie-Q's tiny chest moving up and down reassuring, too.

She chuckled a humorless sound. "Thank you for not laughing at me. I know I'm being silly over just an ear infection."

"It's never wrong for a mother to worry about her baby. What's wrong is for a mother not to care."

"Like Scotty's mother?"

"Like all the boys here."

She lifted her head from his shoulder. "Is that why you ended up here, too?"

"My mother deserted me in a grocery store when I was ten. After a while I got hungry and snitched an ice-cream bar. One of the clerks spotted me and the rest, as they say, is history." He couldn't even remember his birth father, only a series of his mother's boyfriends and finally the one she had married—a guy who hadn't wanted Walker around.

She palmed his cheek, caressing him with her thumb. "I'm so sorry. I can't imagine how a mother could do that to a child."

"It's all right. It happened a long time ago." Except that sometimes he could remember that day as clearly as if it were yesterday, all the pain and fear coming back in a rush. "But it does mean I'm the last person on earth who's going to give you a hard time about loving your baby."

"I do love her. More than my own life." With a sigh, she rested her head against his shoulder again. "My family was so, I don't know, cold. I don't want Susie-Q to be raised like that."

"She won't be. Not with you as her mom."

He held Lizzie on his lap, stroking her hair. The color reminded him of the silvery mane of a golden Palomino he'd once ridden but the strands were softer, like silk, and he toyed with the tips of those that had come loose from her twist. He wanted this moment, and more like it, to go on forever. But he still had questions. Lots of them.

"Lizzie, honey, do you know a man named Pettigrew?"

"Hmm, I don't think so."

"Then why do you suppose the license plates for Mr. Pettigrew's Jeep, which he totaled a few months ago, are on your BMW?"

She stiffened and went very still. Then she slowly exhaled. "I stole the plates from the Jeep in a junkyard."

"Why?"

"I didn't want my family tracking me down."

"And that's the same reason you've been using a false name."

Her head came up. "What makes you think that?"

"When you filled out the forms for Dr. Justine, you wrote down Suzanne Tilden, not Thomas."

"Oh."

"I assume it's the Tilden family that you're running away from and that they're very wealthy."

"Andrew and Dorthea Tilden of Marin, California. Definitely upper crust, country-club set."

"And the man you were about to marry?"

"Vernon Sprague of the Boston Spragues. Likewise upper class and politically powerful. He's a close friend of my brother's and my family has practically adopted him."

"Which is why you didn't think your parents would support your decision to cancel the wedding."

"That's about the size of it."

"No other deep, dark secrets I ought to know about."

Her forehead creased. "Only that I had to repeat kindergarten because I was so shy I didn't play well with the other children, and I cried almost every day at school. I suspect my mother couldn't hold up her head for months after that with her country club friends."

"Your mother should have been more worried about you than her own friends."

Lizzie lifted an unconcerned shoulder. "That's just who she is."

Thoughtfully he reached for one of the sandwiches he'd fixed, offered her a bite then took one himself. The lacy curtains on the window fluttered in a light breeze, stirring the air in the room. A few scattered clouds had appeared in the sky but not enough to produce a decent rain shower. At best, they'd get a few sprinkles. Worst case, dry lightning would start a grass fire, turning the parched landscape black.

If only the drought would break, Walker would be able to relax.

"You probably ought to call your folks to let them know you're all right," he said.

"I called Mother a couple of days after I arrived here. I used my cell phone so they couldn't trace your number."

"If you've got a phone, I'm surprised she isn't calling you every day." Badgering her to come home.

"She may be doing just that but I turned off my phone. I'm not ready to go back yet."

Walker didn't want her to leave, either. But she would. What woman could resist living the high life with fancy clothes, luxury cars and money to burn? How could a man ask her to give up all that for a life of hard work on an isolated ranch?

Elizabeth shifted on Walker's lap. For all practical purposes, she'd cut herself off from her family. She was here in Walker's arms, relishing the feel of him holding her, and that's exactly where she wanted to be. As long as he'd let her.

Lifting her head, she took another bite of the bologna and cheese sandwich he offered her. She chewed slowly, tasting the heavy helping of mustard he'd applied and watching him do the same. He was a beautiful man in every way she could imagine—caring and empathetic yet impossibly strong and masculine.

There was something very sensual about eating while sitting on a man's lap. She felt the flex of his thigh muscles when he moved, experienced each breath he drew as his chest expanded. Up close, she could see the faint stubble of his dark whiskers, the golden flecks nearly hidden in his brown eyes, the perfect shape of his lips. Kissable lips, she remembered so clearly.

But most of all, she was keenly aware of his arousal pressing against her thigh and her own building desire.

"The boys should be back soon from the potluck." He wiped at the corner of her lips with his fingertip. "Mustard."

A shiver rode down her spine, and she nodded. "I hope they got enough to eat."

"They're pretty good about scarfing up anything that's eatable."

"Typical boys, I suppose."

As though pulled by some unseen force, their heads drew closer until their lips were only inches apart. She held her breath. Waiting. Hoping. Dreaming impossible dreams as his eyes darkened to nearly black.

Suzanne cooed a happy, wakeful sound.

Elizabeth shot to her feet as though getting caught in the act by her daughter—Steve's baby—had triggered springs in her knees. Guilty heat flushed her cheeks.

"Hi, sweetie, how are you feeling? Oh, look, she's smiling."

Walker's hand warmed the small of her back as he joined her standing beside the crib. "Looks like Dr. Justine's medicine has already begun to work."

"Thank goodness." Filled with relief, she caressed the baby's forehead and found it cool to the touch. "Her fever's down, too."

Downstairs, the back door banged followed by shouting voices.

"Guess the boys are back," Walker said.

"Sounds like."

He turned her and lifted her chin. A wry smile curled his lips. "Timing is everything, isn't it?"

No need for her to play coy. She knew exactly what he was talking about, exactly what would have happened if Suzanne hadn't picked that particular moment to wake up.

It was hard to know if Suzanne had saved her from a foolish mistake because this time Elizabeth didn't think they would have stopped with a kiss. Or had the interruption only delayed the inevitable?

"Guess I'd better get downstairs before they turn the house into shambles," Walker said.

"I'll change Susie-Q and come down in a minute." Which would give her time to redo her hair and regain some small part of her equilibrium.

She breathed a sigh of relief—or regret, she didn't know which—when Walker left the room. Her body was still trembling in anticipation of his kiss. Still aching for the caresses that surely would have followed. Never in her life, not even with Steve, had she so wanted a man to hold her, love her. It was as though all this fresh Montana air had given a boost to her libido, except she knew darn well the infusion of hormones was the direct result of moving in with a sexy cowboy she couldn't quit dreaming about.

With Steve, everything had seemed so easy. So natural that they'd become a couple and eventually their relationship would become intimate. But *never* had she felt the toe-curling desire she did simply thinking about the prospect of kissing Walker.

A few minutes later—a cheerful, well-diapered baby in her arms—Elizabeth found Speed in the kitchen fixing himself a cup of coffee.

"I brought your potato salad bowl back, Miss Lizzie."

She noted it sitting on the counter, empty. "How much did you have to dump out?"

"Dump out?" Slowly he stirred cream into his coffee then added two teaspoons of sugar. "That bowl was plum clean as a whistle, ma'am. Everybody said it was the best potato salad they'd tasted in ages. I sure know I thought so."

Amazement and no small sense of pride swept through her. "Why, thank you, Speed. I think that's the nicest compliment I've ever received."

It didn't matter that the competing potato salads all left something to be desired. With her own hands, she'd produced a potluck dish that others had enjoyed. Given her lack of experience in the culinary arts, that's what she'd call a major accomplishment.

Even better than finally graduating in a cap and gown from kindergarten.

AFTER MORE THAN A WEEK of riding almost daily, Elizabeth's muscles had grown accustomed to the exercise. With Walker's permission, she'd asked Scotty to watch Suzanne for an hour or so each morning, giving her the freedom to tour the ranch. She relished the opportunity to release some of the pent-up tension that had been building since her near kiss with Walker.

She'd had no idea how hard it would be to live in the same house with a man with whom she wanted to make love.

To her surprise, Chicago had asked to come riding with her this morning. He hadn't talked much, which was another surprise. She'd fully expected him to announce he was planning to leave again but he hadn't said a word.

They'd returned to the ranch, unsaddled their mounts and were grooming them in the shade of the barn. Bandit, who'd become her regular companion on their morning excursions, curled up a safe distance away to watch their efforts.

"How come you don't get your boyfriend to do this stuff for you?" Chicago asked. With little enthusiasm, he brushed Devil Wind's chestnut coat.

She raised her brows. "Boyfriend?"

"Yeah, you know. The boss."

"I don't know what gave you that idea."

"Man, I've seen him look at you. He's so hot to get into your—"

"Chicago." She warned him in a scolding voice. "You've brushed Devil Wind's coat enough for now. How about cleaning his hooves?" She handed him the pick she'd used on Tillamook.

"Jeez, I hate doing that."

"The first thing a cowboy learns is to take care of his horse."

"Nobody asked me if I wanted to be a cowboy. I don't even like riding."

"But you're getting much better at it."

He looked startled by her comment. "You think?"

"It's not an easy thing to learn to control twelve hundred pounds of horseflesh. You're doing fine."

"Bean Pole thinks I stink."

She eyed him skeptically. "And you believed him?" she teased.

"Naw, I knew he was putting me on."

Thoughtfully he lifted Devil Wind's right rear leg and started to clean his hoof. "Guess you didn't tell the boss about me trying to steal his money, huh?"

"I told him. He *is* responsible for you and needed to know you were thinking about running away."

"You told him about the money and stuff? How come he didn't send me back to the county?"

"I think he has more faith in you than you have in yourself and believes you deserve another chance."

Returning to his silent mood, Chicago managed only a halfhearted job of the first hoof then went on to the next. Although Elizabeth had finished grooming her horse, she lingered. She didn't think the boy was through talking yet.

Finally he looked up. "I've been thinking…"

She waited attentively, giving him the chance to say what was on his mind.

"This place ain't so bad, once you get used to it. I figure I'll stay a while. Till something better comes along, I mean."

She desperately wanted to hug the boy but imagined

that would be more affection than he could handle at the moment. He'd been so badly scarred by his past, it would be a long time before he would trust that another adult actually cared about him.

"I'm glad," she said simply. "Walker will be, too."

"Yeah. Whatever." The boy shrugged but behind that careless gesture she could see his relief. She understood that everyone, no matter their age, was in search of a place they could call home.

Elizabeth was no exception.

HE'D START CULLING THE HERD tomorrow. Even if rain did come, the grass was too thin to support as many head as he had grazing on the land. He'd start with fifty head from the west pasture.

Walker called a trucking company to arrange trailer transportation. He and Speed, with the help of the boys—and his brothers, if he could reach them—could get the animals separated and penned in a temporary corral in the morning. The trucks would show up later in the day.

And he'd take his losses.

Discouraged, he went outside to find Speed. Instead he found Lizzie leading Tillamook back to the corral after her morning ride. Her sweet smile lifted his spirits.

"You have a good time today?" he asked.

She looked up at him from under his old battered straw hat. He really ought to buy her a new one, maybe one with a fancy bow or something.

"Chicago came along with me this morning."

"Yeah?"

"He wanted to tell me he's planning to stay a while."

"That a fact?" He opened the corral gate for her, pleased with the news. "I was hoping he'd settle in."

"You know something else?" She gave the horse an affectionate swat on his rump, then stood aside while Walker latched the gate closed.

"He's in love with you?" Walker wouldn't blame the boy, but he'd also tan his hide good if the kid had made a move on Lizzie.

She tossed her head like an arrogant filly who knew exactly what she wanted. "Quite possibly, I suppose. But if he is, it's only childish infatuation, like a crush on a favorite teacher."

"Don't let him hear you say that."

"I won't." She grinned at him and leaned back against the rail fence. "The thing is, talking with Frankie and the other boys, I realize now I *should* have followed my heart as I was growing up."

As far as Walker was concerned, Lizzie had grown up as good as a woman could get. Intelligent. Easy to talk to. Breasts the perfect size for cupping in his palms, hips meant to nestle against his.

"I should have gone on to get my master's in social work," she continued with a determined nod. "Over my parents' objections, if I had to. Even if they wouldn't pay for my schooling, I could have used my grandmother's trust fund to cover my expenses."

"You have a trust fund?"

She tilted her head, looking surprised he'd asked. Like maybe everyone she knew had a trust fund squirreled away somewhere.

"Not a huge one but enough to live off for a year or two. And if I'd done that, I might have been doing something productive by now and I wouldn't have agreed so easily to a loveless marriage."

"So that's what you've decided to do?" His chest tightened the way it used to when he got on a bronc at a rodeo, hoping to hang on for eight seconds. Unlike Eric, who'd been a champion rider until he was injured, Walker had rarely lasted that long.

"Do?"

"Go back to school."

"Oh, well…I hadn't thought that far ahead yet." Frowning as though considering the possibility for the first time, she shoved away from the fence. "I'd better go rescue Scotty. Or maybe it's Susie-Q who needs rescuing. That boy spoils her to pieces."

"He is real fond of the baby."

"I think it's because he misses his mother and baby sister so much. He's trying to make up for whatever imagined wrong he did that caused his mother to desert him."

"It will never be enough." Walker knew that from experience. For years he'd searched for that one mistake he'd made, the one sin he'd committed, that had sent his mother away. He'd never found the answer. She'd simply walked away from him.

Lizzie was going to walk away, too, not just back into the house.

She was going to walk out of his life. The realization hurt so much, it felt like he'd taken a punch to his gut. He could barely breathe.

He'd known all along she'd leave him. But he'd thought she'd be going back to some rich society life; not going to school.

That would be her choice. He knew it deep in his soul.

Damn! There wasn't a college around here for hundreds of miles. If a kid from Grass Valley wanted an education beyond high school, he moved away. Walker had chosen not to go, despite his dad's urging.

Lizzie wouldn't make that same decision. She had no roots to tie her here, no love of the land.

He was going to lose her. To her family. Or because she wanted an education. The reason didn't matter.

And he cursed himself for wanting things to be different. For wanting a woman to choose him over everything else.

"Ain't gonna happen," he muttered under his breath remembering his high school sweetheart, who he had hoped to marry after they had both graduated. Instead she'd gone to New York to sing on stage. The last he'd heard, she'd married a waiter who wanted to be a Broadway dancer and they were expecting their second child.

Nope. Whatever flaw his mother had detected meant he was still standing at the back of the line.

THE MASHED POTATES WERE still lumpy. For the life of her, Elizabeth couldn't figure out how to make the potatoes as creamy as Scotty had managed that first night she arrived at the ranch. She'd have to ask him.

"Dinner's ready!" she called to the boys, who were in the living room watching television.

They came running like a cattle stampede, pushing and shoving for position. She smiled at the memory of how overly polite they'd been those first few nights, even gagging down her dreadful cooking.

Fridge landed in his chair with a thud. "Roast beef and gravy. That's great!"

"Burned biscuits, too," she said, setting the plate on the table. "Sorry about that. I forgot to set the timer." Suzanne had made a soggy mess of her shirt spitting up, and she'd had to take the baby upstairs to change her clothes, entirely forgetting she'd put the biscuits in the oven.

"A little charcoal won't hurt these tough guys," Speed said, giving her a wink.

She'd have to consult with Speed on the biscuits, too. Even on her best day, hers weren't as light and fluffy as his. But she didn't usually burn them quite so badly.

Seating herself, she glanced in Walker's direction and was snared by the troubled look in his dark eyes. She hadn't seen him since their morning conversation and she wondered if Frankie had said or done something wrong. From the way the boy was piling food on his plate, though, the youngster didn't appear worried.

After dinner, when the boys went back to the bunkhouse, she'd ask Walker what was wrong.

She'd just reached for the bowl of string beans with bacon bits when she felt the shaking begin. At first she only felt it on her rear end. Then the dishes on the table started to rattle and so did the ones in the cupboard. Overhead, the light fixture began to sway.

"Okay, whoever is rocking the table, cut it out," Walker ordered.

Their eyes widening, the boys looked at each other. Speed halted his glass of milk in midair, halfway between the table and his mouth.

Elizabeth grabbed for the plate of biscuits that was dancing toward the edge of the table. "It's not one of the boys, Walker. It's an earthquake." A reasonably strong one, based on her memories of San Francisco, but nothing to be afraid of. Unless it kept going too long.

Bean Pole was up first. "I'm getting outta here—" He took a header over Fridge's leg as he was trying to exit the premises, too.

Scotty scrambled out of his chair to throw his body protectively over Suzanne, who was in her car seat. Frankie headed for the back door.

Within seconds, only Elizabeth and Walker were still sitting at the table. She grinned at him as the motion of the earth slowed.

"It's over guys," she said. "Relax."

From his position on his knees, Speed reached up to put his still full glass of milk on the table. "That was pretty interesting," he drawled.

"I didn't know you had earthquakes in Montana,"

Elizabeth commented, unconcerned with the roller they'd experienced.

Looking relieved the shaking had stopped, Walker shrugged. "We don't often. They had a big one down toward Yellowstone some years ago. Caused a whole lot of damage and brought down a mountain, which dammed up a river. That made a mess of some of the campgrounds, flooding them."

Chagrined by his pratfall, Bean Pole slipped back into his chair. "How come you weren't scared?" he asked Elizabeth.

"I'm a native Californian. You get kind of used to earthquakes, and as long as you're not near the epicenter, you just ride them out."

"I don't think I wanna ride no more of them things anytime soon," Frankie said, and they all laughed.

Despite jangled nerves, the boys began eating again. Adolescent appetites weren't put on hold simply because of a little rockin' and rollin'.

They'd about finished the meal when Walker revealed what was troubling him.

"We're going to start culling the herd tomorrow," he said.

"What's that mean?" Frankie asked.

"It means we're going to pick out about fifty head from the west pasture and ship them to the meat packing plant in Chester."

The youngster looked stunned by the announcement. "You're gonna kill 'em?"

"Have to. The grass is drying out so fast, there won't be enough for the rest to graze if we don't cut down the size of the herd. The ones that are left won't fatten up and won't be worth peanuts at auction this fall.''

"Jeez, that's cold, killin' your own cows.''

"We don't slaughter them here, Chicago. We round them up and ship them in trailers.''

"You gonna take the babies, too?'' He seemed particularly concerned about the young animals.

"Mostly the older cows, particularly those that didn't have calves this season.'' Walker looked around the table. ''I'll need all of you boys to help with the roundup. My brothers are coming, too. At least Eric is. Rory may not be able to get away. It's going to be dirty and dusty work.''

Obviously he meant for Elizabeth and Suzanne to stay at home. She had other plans, however.

The phone rang in the other room.

Walker rose from his place at the head of the table. ''I'll get it. But keep in mind tomorrow is likely to be a long day. Get some rest tonight.''

He left and when he returned a few minutes later he looked doubly grim.

"That was Eric calling from town. There's been a landslide and it dammed up the Sage River.''

"It's practically dry anyway,'' Speed commented.

"It's going to be dryer on our end if we don't do something about it. That would mean the cows in the north pasture won't get anything to drink. And if whatever we do comes out wrong, it'll flood the whole damn town.''

Without being told what was needed, Speed shoved back from the table. "I'll come into town with you."

Suddenly the room was filled with action, the boys shoving their plates aside and getting their hats. Nobody was going to be left behind.

Including Elizabeth.

Chapter Nine

"You can't climb up on top of all those rocks and stick a piece of dynamite in there!"

Standing beside Walker's truck with Suzanne safely napping inside, Elizabeth gaped at the mound of earth that now dammed the river a half-mile downstream from town, turning the downstream side into little more than a trickle. Upstream, behind the jumble of rocks and debris, water rose to form a lake that would soon threaten Grass Valley. The plan the townspeople had proposed to blow apart the dam sounded impossibly dangerous.

"If we don't, the Double O will dry up."

"You could be killed!"

"Joe Moore, Hetty's husband, used to work in the mines before he opened the general store. He knows what he's doing."

"But do you?"

"Let's hope I'm a fast learner."

That wasn't in the least reassuring. "Why does it have to be you? Why couldn't someone else—"

"I just told you. Without the river running through

the ranch, the cows don't have a reliable source of water during a drought like this year. I'm responsible for the Double O. That's my job.''

His *passion,* she realized. Nothing in the world was more important to Walker than the Double O.

Real terror, heart-palpitating fear, coursed through her veins. All she could see was Walker blown apart limb by limb, his beautiful body destroyed by the force of the explosion, bits of him shot skyward only to fall back to earth in a heart-sickening rain of death.

She shuddered. Dear God, she couldn't lose him. Not when she'd never had the chance to love him.

"If you get yourself killed, what will happen to the boys?" *What will happen to me? To the refuge she'd sought?* She tried to keep the panic out of her voice, the pleading. "And the ranch? Speed can't run it—"

"Eric and Rory own shares in the ranch. They'd inherit my share.''

"Wonderful! That's assuming *they* aren't killed, too. I'm so glad you have everything worked out.'' She struggled against the tears that flooded her eyes. Damn it all! If he didn't care about risking his fool neck, why should she? It's not like they had any kind of an understanding. One kiss plus a near miss didn't count as a relationship.

He tugged her into his arms, and she buried her face against his chest. He smelled of fabric softener and horseflesh, a uniquely masculine scent when combined with his own.

"Shh, it's all right, Slick. I promise I won't get myself blown up.''

"Men always break their promises." Her father had always sworn he'd be home for her birthdays or her graduation, one event or another. Special days that he'd missed because he'd been too busy earning money or playing golf at the country club, which was the same thing according to him. As an adolescent, she'd sworn that once she married Steve she'd never allow a golf club in her house.

But the fact was, he'd had an eight handicap. Vernon's scores were even better, and he did most of his business on the links at the country club. Why in God's name had she thought she'd be happy married to a man so much like her father? And her brother, Robert, wasn't much different. Though she dearly loved her brother, he'd rather play a round of golf or go tooling around the Bay in his boat than concentrate on his law practice.

But at the moment, she'd trade Walker a stick of dynamite for a golf club if it would keep him safe.

"It's not my way to break a promise," he whispered, rubbing his cheek across the top of her head.

Instinctively she knew that was true. He was a man who took his responsibilities seriously. A man of his word. A good man with a warm heart and a strong body.

She wrapped her arms around him and held on tight, hoping that what little strength she had would be added to his.

It didn't matter that virtually every member of the community was standing around on a knoll above the river waiting for Joe Moore to return with some dynamite. Elizabeth didn't care if everyone was gawking at them. She simply cherished Walker's embrace and never wanted to give it up.

"You know I won't forgive you if you blow yourself into tiny bits, don't you?"

She felt more than heard a chuckle rumble through his chest. "I'll use that to motivate me to be extra careful."

"See that you do."

THE TOWNSPEOPLE GREW HUSHED as they watched the four men gingerly make their way across the boulders that blocked the river. Three adopted brothers and a man too old to be climbing where one misstep could cause an avalanche, burying them all beneath tons of dirt and rocks.

Even the boys from the ranch were quiet, having joined up with their friends, all of the adolescents respectful of the danger and heroics they were witnessing.

Ready in case she was needed, Dr. Justine stood nearby, her doctor's bag perched on the hood of her truck. Elizabeth would have preferred a full-fledged emergency medical team and an army of rescue workers. Towns like Grass Valley didn't have the benefit of such sophisticated municipal services.

Montana grew a tough, independent breed of men and women. They were on their own. A terrifying thought if anything went wrong.

Elizabeth wasn't sure she'd ever have the grit these townspeople took in stride.

Although it was well after dinnertime, this far north the summer sun was still fairly high in the sky and wouldn't set for another two hours. Despite the warm evening air, Elizabeth shivered and tugged her light sweater more snugly around her shoulders.

Hetty stood beside her. "Don't you worry, now. They'll be fine. My Joe knows what he's doing."

"I hope so."

Lending their moral support, the church ladies gathered around them.

"Those Oakes boys, even though they were wild ones when they were young, always showed a lot of spunk," Abby Treadwell said.

"Grew into fine men, they did," Marlene Huhn assured her.

"Fine men," Valery Haywood echoed, although her tone sounded as worried as Elizabeth felt. "I thought sure my girl and Walker would get together but I guess it wasn't meant to be. They were so cute together in high school."

Without taking her eyes off of Walker, Elizabeth asked, "Walker dated your daughter?"

"Oh, more than that. They were quite an item. Of course, she moved away and is married now but I do wish she'd stayed here. Would have been nice to see my grandbabies more often."

My God, Walker had loved and lost, too. She should have realized—

She gasped as she saw his foot slip on a rock and he had to steady himself to regain his balance. A fine shower of dirt slid down to puddle in the nearly dry riverbed.

How long could she hold her breath, she wondered. For a minute? For five minutes?

Ignoring Valery, she took Hetty's hand and squeezed hard. Together they'd hold their breath forever if that's what it took to bring their men back safely.

USING A LONG METAL ROD, Walker poked a hole in the loose dirt beneath one of the larger boulders near the center of the riverbed. Joe had talked about the need to split apart the keystone. If that went, the whole dam would go and the river would be able to flow again.

Walker just hoped nothing blew while he was standing up close and personal with a ten-ton rock.

A few feet away, Eric was working on the opposite side of the same boulder. "You ask Lizzie about that license plate?"

"Yep."

"She have a good answer?"

"Good enough for me."

Easing the stick of dynamite into the hole he'd reamed, Walked used the rod to gently tamp it farther under the boulder, hoping to God he didn't hit it too hard.

"You got something going with her?" Eric asked.

"She's not planning to stay long."

"You want her to?"

As much as a man wanted to breathe. "Yeah."

"Then what are you going to do about it?"

"What do you mean?"

Eric sat back, balancing himself on the balls of his feet, one hand on the rock face. "How are you going to change her mind about staying?"

"It's not my choice." No matter what he did, Lizzie would leave. A city slicker like her with a bunch of other choices wasn't likely to hang around the Double O. Not through the heat of summer and on into the blizzards of winter. Not year after year. Oliver Oakes had found that out the hard way.

Hell, half the women who were raised here didn't want to stay.

Rory came scrambling toward them from the spot where he'd planted his dynamite. "If you don't want to encourage Lizzie to stay, I'd be interested in trying. Been thinking about coming to call again anyway."

Reflexively Walker gave the rod an extra hard whack. He winced, waiting for an explosion that didn't come. "No need. There haven't been any new cases of pinkeye in weeks."

Rory laughed at him.

Walker would have laughed, too, except the thought of Lizzie leaving wasn't funny.

"Seems to me, Sharpy," Eric said, "you're a man with considerable charm when you want to use it. Why don't you apply your talents to getting her to stick around for a while?"

"Good idea," Rory agreed. "Once she gets to know him, I'll look that much better to her."

Tempted to toss his brother off his precarious perch,

Walker thought better of it. The least little thing could bring down the entire wall of rock they were standing on. Better to get even with Rory later.

It would be better yet if Walker found a way to convince Lizzie to stay with him. He wasn't sure any man had that much charm, whatever his brother claimed.

But he had been known to do a fair job of courting a woman when he put his mind to it, which hadn't been often. He might just give it a try again. What did he have to lose?

Walker edged back across the strewn boulders with his brothers, making their way to where Joe was waiting to attach the lead wires from the sticks of dynamite they'd planted to the single wire he'd run to the detonator. Stringing out the coil of wire behind them, they all eased off the landslide and up onto the knoll above the town.

"Move everybody away from the river," Joe told them as he crouched down beside the detonator. "If this thing blows like it should, we could have rocks flying from here to Boise."

Happy to follow Joe's instructions, Walker urged the townspeople to move back out of harm's way.

When he got to Lizzie, she stepped right into his arms as if she belonged there. He didn't even consider arguing with her.

"Miss me?" he asked with a grin.

"You macho jerk. I was scared out of my wits the whole time you were out there showing off."

"So you were worried, huh?"

She trembled against him, and he absorbed the sensation, wanting to feel her trembling again for another reason.

"Fire in the hole!" Joe shouted. He waited a second then pushed the plunger on the detonator.

An eerie silence followed while nothing seemed to happen, an odd stillness where everyone appeared to be holding their breath. Even the evening birds had grown quiet in anticipation. Walker kept his eye on the boulder where he'd placed his charge.

Slowly, almost imperceptibly, the mammoth rock began to rise. An instant later a rapid series of *whomps* echoed across the landscape. Dirt and rock erupted into the air. Dust exploded, shrouding the view of the river in an impenetrable cloud. Instinctively everyone stepped back a few more paces.

To Walker's dismay, when the cloud of dust dissipated, the wall of rock was still there blocking the river, big boulders now smaller ones. But as he watched, a trickle of water oozed out from under the natural dam, the trickle quickly turning into a torrent that shoved rocks and dirt aside. The gap widened and deepened, soon becoming a foaming river of dirt and mud and rocks rushing downstream toward the Double O grazing land and his thirsty cows.

A huge cheer went up from the crowd.

Walker took advantage of the distraction and kissed Lizzie, claiming the kiss just the way he wanted it to be—long and hard, deliberately sensual and as carnal as he could without causing a riot among the townspeople. A kiss meant to persuade and tempt. He gave it his all.

Her hand rested on his chest, her fingers curling into his shirt like an eager feline, and she made a low throaty sound of pleasure.

Her avid response nearly sent him over the edge, putting him at risk of doing something really foolish in front of the entire population of Grass Valley. Including his brothers.

He eased back, as shaken by his reaction as though he'd experienced an aftershock from the earthquake.

Rory slapped him on the back. "We're all going to the saloon to celebrate. You coming?"

He eyed Lizzie, who had jumped away from Walker the moment Rory showed up, damn his timing.

"Or do you two have something better to do?" Rory asked slyly.

The sound of Susie-Q crying in the back seat of the truck answered the question.

Flushed, Lizzie glanced in that direction. "I'd better take Suzanne back to the ranch. You go ahead, Walker. You deserve a celebration. I can drive the truck home and Speed will give you a ride when you're ready."

"Nope, I'll take you home now."

"You'll be missing a big party," Rory insisted. "George says the first round is on the house."

"Catch you later, Bird Brain," he muttered to his brother then slipped his arm possessively around Lizzie's shoulders. They walked to the truck.

"You sure you don't want to stay?" she asked.

"Positive." No man could be a hundred percent confident about what any woman was thinking. But if Lizzie's response to his kiss meant anything, Walker was damn well hoping to enjoy a private celebration with her in his bed.

Elizabeth picked Suzanne up out of her car seat, lifting the baby to her shoulder.

"Did all that noise wake you up, honey bunch?" she crooned, patting the infant's back, consoling her. "It's all right. Mommy's here now."

Holding the baby, she met Walker's gaze. Fear-fed adrenaline still pumped through her veins. His kiss had accelerated the flow, like the river breaking through the dam. And her pulse pounded in her throat.

His eyes were so dark, his touch so possessive, she knew when they got back to the ranch he'd make love to her. Despite her swirling excitement and her aching need for him, that realization terrified her almost as much as watching him risk his life crawling across the landslide had.

It had been more than a year since she'd last made love. Her intimacies with Steve had been loving but inexperienced, less than successful or satisfying. She was sure Walker would be a far more demanding lover than he had been.

And more skilled.

She *wasn't* sure she'd be able to keep up. To satisfy him.

To make matters worse, she hadn't regained her figure since her pregnancy. Her poochy tummy and stretch marks were all too apparent when she stood naked in front of a mirror.

She wasn't sure she had enough nerve to have Walker see her that way.

Panic, the fear of failure or rejection, warred with her desire. Her good sense appeared to have deserted her altogether and she desperately tried to call it back into play. "Look, you shouldn't miss all the fun just because I'm stuck with a baby. You, Joe and your brothers are the heroes of the day."

The back of his hand skimmed down her cheek in a slow caress. "I don't intend to miss all the fun."

Under some other circumstances, the gesture might have been chaste. But not now. Instead his touch sent a lightning bolt of heat right to her feminine core.

"Are you afraid of me?" he asked.

"No. Of course not." More likely she was afraid of herself. Afraid of disappointing them both.

"Great. Then let's get Susie-Q home where she belongs."

SUZANNE DIDN'T WANT TO GO to sleep.

She wanted to play. She wanted to fuss. But sleep was way down on her agenda.

It was just as well, Elizabeth told herself as she picked the baby up the second time from her crib to carry her back downstairs.

"It's hopeless," she said as she returned to the living room.

Walker stood, holding out his hands to take the baby. He'd showered while she'd been trying to get the baby to sleep and his hair was still damp. "You think she's sick again?"

Happily Suzanne went into his arms making gurgling noises to tell him how glad she was to be out of her crib hanging around with the man of the house.

"She doesn't have a fever. I checked."

He lifted the baby in the air. She stretched and laughed out loud. "Looks like she wants to go sky-diving."

"That's Scotty's fault. His latest stunt with the baby."

"She's not rubbing her ear like she did in Dr. Justine's office, so the medicine's still working."

"My best guess is she had too long a nap in the truck after dinner. It'll be midnight before she goes down again."

Raising his brows, he caught the baby in the crook of his arm. "Miss Susie-Q, I think you and I ought to have a serious talk. There are times when your mother might like to do something besides hang out with you. Now, don't take offense—" He brushed a quick kiss to her forehead. "But moms do have lives of their own. You gotta give her a break."

"Walker, I know you thought…and I thought, too, we might, you know…when we got back here."

He slanted her a curious glance. "You're having second thoughts?"

"Well, I…" She picked up a pillow one of the boys had left on the floor while watching TV before dinner and tossed it back onto the couch. "I haven't, I mean it's been a long time since I, long before the baby—"

"You think you're still tender?"

"I don't know." Her chin trembled and her cheeks flushed at having such an intimate conversation. She wanted him to get on with it without so much conversation; she wanted to flee from the room, not do this at all. "I haven't even thought—"

"If you don't want to, we don't have to do anything. It's okay."

She saw the hunger in his eyes, the need that matched her own. "No, it's not okay. I shouldn't have, I don't know—led you on."

He eased closer to her, rocking the baby in his arms. "Maybe I came on too strong. I didn't mean to frighten you with that kiss."

"No, it's not that." But it was—partly. As well as his incredible masculinity. He simply overpowered her with his utter maleness. She'd never met anyone like Walker before and certainly hadn't slept with a man as potent as he was. He'd give a good many women stronger and more confident than Elizabeth palpations, she was sure. And yet he wanted her.

That realization astonished her.

"Good, because I like kissing you." To demonstrate, he lowered his head to slant a kiss across her mouth, first one way then the other, slowly, as though he were in no rush at all. "You taste good."

She shuddered. "You do, too."

He did it again, this time kissing her at the sensitive

spot right beneath her ear. "I like the way you smell. Violets and baby powder. Very feminine."

She smiled as her breath snagged in her lungs. "When you've been out riding or working around the ranch, you smell of horses and leather. Very masculine. Now you smell fresh, like summer." And desirable.

He nuzzled the opposite side of her throat. "Works out well, doesn't it, that you're a girl and I'm a boy."

Not a boy but a very competent, seductive man.

"Suzanne has fallen asleep," Elizabeth whispered.

His gaze followed hers to the sleeping baby in his arms, and his lips quirked with the hint of a smile. "I thought having a heart-to-heart with her would help."

"Magical."

"How 'bout we take her upstairs?"

If Elizabeth agreed, it meant she'd have to face the moment of truth sooner rather than later. Her courage faltered. "She might wake up again as soon as we put her down."

"I'm willing to risk it."

"I'm not all that good at—"

"This isn't a test, Lizzie."

With his free arm, he ushered her toward the stairs. The steps seemed incredibly long and steep, her legs heavy, leaving her breathless by the time they reached the upstairs hallway. In the nursery, the night-light glowed orange, keeping most of the room in shadows.

Gingerly, as though he were handling a precious piece of artwork, he lay the baby down in the crib. She didn't so much as make a peep.

"A man of many talents," Elizabeth said.

"I hope so." With the same care he'd used with the baby, he slipped the light sweater she was wearing off her shoulders and down her arms, his callused hands skimming across her flesh. Deliberately, watching her with quiet intensity, he folded the sweater, draping it over the side of the crib. "If I do anything you don't like, or if I hurt you in any way, you let me know, okay?"

That would require her to retain some small ability to speak. The band around Elizabeth's chest was drawn so tightly, she could barely breathe much less utter a coherent sound.

With painstaking care, he started to undo the buttons that ran down the front of her sundress. "I like zippers but buttons are more of a challenge."

The back of his hand brushed against her breast and she gasped. "You like rising to the occasion, huh?"

His fingers came to an abrupt halt on the third button. "Slick? Are you making jokes when I'm trying to seduce you?"

"No. I mean, I wasn't even thinking about that."

"Well, *start* thinking about it."

The top of her dress gaped open and he cupped her breasts, weighing them in his wide palm. His thumb brushed the rigid tips with electrifying effect.

"Walker, I..." She moaned, unable to finish the thought.

"I think we've convinced Susie-Q to stay down for a while. How 'bout we continue this where we can be a little more comfortable?"

Since her legs were about to collapse beneath her, Elizabeth thought that was a perfect idea. Indeed, she was ready to follow Walker Oakes wherever he wanted to lead her.

Chapter Ten

Taking her hand, he led her across the hall to his bedroom, where he switched on a table lamp next to an impossibly large bed. Perfect for a man Walker's size but one that would engulf Elizabeth. The bed was neatly made, the summer-weight spread pulled up to cover a row of three king-size pillows.

Everything about the room seemed expansive and blatantly masculine. A leather recliner. A dark walnut desk almost as large as the one in Walker's office downstairs. A heavy chest of drawers in matching wood. Nothing showed the signs of a woman's touch, no vase to be filled with flowers from the garden, no family pictures on the walls. Nothing to soften the impact of Walker's virility.

Feeling vulnerable, Elizabeth shivered.

"There's nothing to be afraid of."

"I know." That wasn't entirely true but she wanted it to be.

"I want you, Lizzie."

His eyes were so deep, his expression so intense, she felt a responding desire building more potently within her than she'd ever before experienced. *Lizzie,* this new person she was becoming, could do this. Could match him need for need, passion for passion. Lizzie had no past, no reason to feel guilty about loving a virile cowboy. That new awareness freed her in ways nothing else could have.

"I want you, too." Reaching up to him, she claimed his mouth in the same way he had earlier claimed hers. A rough sound, almost like a growl, rumbled up from his chest, as he responded to her assertive demands. His heated reaction bolstered her confidence, encouraged her to continue her voyage of discovery. With building excitement, she learned evocative details about Walker—and her own avid responses.

Together their kisses became more urgent. His lips defined the outline of her jaw, the vulnerable column of her neck. In return, she marked his throat with her lips.

More eager than ever, she tugged his shirt from his jeans. He shoved her dress from her shoulders. It gathered at her waist while he released her bra, letting the silken fabric drop to the floor. When he laved her pebbled nipple, she cried out. And then he took it in his mouth.

"Walker, I can't—it's—oh, don't stop."

He couldn't free Lizzie or himself of clothes fast enough. He wanted to learn each sweet curve of her body, the silken feel of her skin in his palms. And wanted her to do the same to him. With each caress, he wanted to brand the sensation into her memory. The memory of him loving her, of him holding her. Entering her.

He fought for control even as he brought her down to the bed with him. Her skin was damp, her taste as sweet as honey. How could he go slowly enough, gently enough not to hurt her? How could his lovemaking be memorable enough that she'd want to live on an isolated ranch for the rest of her life? That she wouldn't abandon him when he'd only just found her, when the taste of her would always be on his tongue.

His fears collided with his desire, feeding the urgent fires burning within him.

"Lizzie! Lizzie!" He moaned.

"I'm here."

But for how long?

To block out the voice of doubt, he covered her face and body with kisses while he probed her welcoming heat, checking her readiness, testing to make sure she wasn't too tender to accept him.

With his last small sense of reason, he rolled away long enough to find a foil packet in the back of his bed table drawer. With shaking hands, he sheathed himself.

When he turned back to her, he feared his moment of caution might have doused her desire. Instead he saw gratitude in her eyes.

"Thank you," she whispered, reaching for him again.

"No need to thank me yet. We're a long way from finished."

Elizabeth skimmed her hands over his chest as he

rose above her and spread her legs with his knees. Barely able to catch her breath, her whole body trembled in anticipation. She'd never been this aroused, this eager, this desperate to find completion in the arms of a man.

She squirmed beneath him, seeking, demanding. "Walker, hurry—"

"I don't want to hurt you—"

"You won't."

Never had anything felt so good. So perfect. With an agonizingly slow stroke, he slid into her damp heat, making them one, and she lifted her hips to meet him. Her body stretched to accept him, and he filled her beyond all imagining. She celebrated their union even as she marveled that such a large man could give her so much pleasure.

He continued to kiss her even as he moved within her. Sure. Confident. Driving her desire ever higher until she teetered on the edge of a precipice.

After that there wasn't much thought at all. Only heat and wanting and a mutual explosion of desire more powerful than a dozen sticks of dynamite.

In a corner of her mind, she realized he'd waited for her to find her ultimate pleasure before he allowed his own release. His control, his generosity and caring overwhelmed her.

His arms buckled, and he collapsed onto her. She cherished the feel of his weight pressing her into the mattress, the sound of his rasping breath that matched her own frantic efforts to draw air into her lungs.

Slowly her heart rate eased. Her breathing returned

to normal, and her sweat-sheened flesh chilled in the cool evening air.

With a groan, he lifted his weight away and pulled her into his arms.

She drifted in a dreamy mist, only half awake. With her head on his shoulder, she could hear the steady beat of his heart, feel the rise and fall of his chest. Lethargy crept through her. It would be so easy to give herself over to this delicious feeling of security. To let herself drift through life with no thought of the future, relying on Walker to take care of her.

Outside, a truck honked a six-tone greeting.

Walker muttered a curse under his breath. "Speed and the boys are back."

Elizabeth shot upright. "I'd better get back to my own room."

"They aren't going to come in the house. They're just letting us know they're home."

He reached for her but she scooted away from his grasp. "I know. I just think it would be better if I slept in my own bed."

Disappointment, sharp and penetrating, lanced through Walker. "Sure. I understand."

Bending over, she brushed a kiss to his cheek. "I'll see you in the morning."

"I'll have to be up early for the roundup. I'll try not to wake you."

"Don't worry about it. Chances are good your Susie-Q will have me up early anyway."

She slipped from the room as silently as a ghost, and a part of him wondered if he'd imagined the whole thing. Wondered if Lizzie was only a dream that would always evaporate with the dawn.

She'd said *your* Susie-Q. He didn't think she realized it. Despite all reason, his heart squeezed with the faint hope her words gave him.

ELIZABETH SCOOPED UP as many bits and pieces of her clothing as she could find, then hurried to her room. Dumping everything in a heap in the closet, she pulled on her nightgown and slid between the cold sheets of her bed.

The irrational fear of getting caught had her heart pounding against her ribs. Her body still hummed from the incredible experience of making love with Walker, her flesh still warm from his touch.

Dear heaven! What was she going to do?

Eyes wide-open, she stared into the darkness, listening to the sounds of night creatures. Crickets chirped an entire symphony beneath her open window. The arms of the elm tree at the front of the house rattled leaves against one another in a breeze so light it barely moved the curtains. Somewhere a cow lowed a lonely sound, and in the distance a wolf called to its mate.

She hadn't come to Montana in search of a man. She'd never intended to stay. A temporary refuge was all she'd been seeking for herself and her baby.

She'd found much more.

But she hadn't yet found herself.

Growing up she had taken the easy route, relying on her family for decisions she should have been making for herself. Relying on Steve to set the pace of their relationship. She'd tried to please everyone. She'd even allowed herself to be lured into believing marriage to Vernon would somehow be the right thing to do, that he was the *perfect* match for her, or so she'd been told over and over.

Until she could lay claim to her own destiny, she didn't dare rely on anyone else.

Even when her heart pleaded otherwise.

CUTTING CATTLE FROM A HERD was an elaborate dance, a horse and rider partnered with a reluctant cow, all of which was accomplished to the accompaniment of bawling animals, resembling a chorus of out-of-tune cellos.

Elizabeth watched at a safe distance from the portable corral the crew had set up in the west pasture. Constructed of fence sections made of pipe, it was designed to funnel the selected cows into a chute where they could be easily loaded onto a trailer for transport to the meat packer.

Spotting her, Walker loped his cow pony in her direction, reined him to a stop beside her. He'd left the house before she awoke, and at the sight of his tentative smile, her heart did a tumble. *Mornings after* could be so darn awkward, and she wasn't at all sure what he was thinking.

Her throat closed down tight as she recognized the only way she'd discover her own future was to leave the Double O—and Walker.

He tipped his hat to the back of his head. Although

it was still early in the day, sweat glistened on his forehead and stained his shirt beneath his arms. "I thought you were going to stay at the ranch house."

"I thought it would be interesting to see a roundup." *Once before I go.*

"It's dirty, dusty work."

"I'm not afraid of a little dirt."

"How about Susie-Q?" He glanced at the baby in her Snugli carrier.

"She loves to ride so much, I'm thinking of signing her up now for equestrian events in the Olympics."

"She could do rodeo barrel racing a lot sooner than that," he countered.

If she stayed in Montana. "I'll ask her which she prefers."

His horse pranced sideways and pulled at his bit, eager to get back to work. With a slight movement, Walker corrected the horse's behavior. "Are you okay? I mean...last night—"

"I'm fine." Except for the acceleration of her heart rate whenever she remembered what he'd done to her—and she'd done to him—and the dreadful ache that filled her chest at the thought of leaving him.

"Good. I wouldn't want you to have any morning-after regrets."

"I don't." The memory would last a lifetime.

A slow, suggestive grin creased his cheeks. "Me, either."

Heat that didn't come from the sun warmed her face, and she laughed. "I'd hate to think I was so awful in bed that you'd be sorry you'd bothered."

"Never," he whispered.

One of the boys shouted something, and Walker looked over his shoulder. "Gotta go. I don't want any of my cows ending up with a broken leg before we even load them in the trailers."

"How long will you be?"

"Trucks come this afternoon. We'll all be back for supper."

"I'll have dinner ready for you." She swallowed hard. "This morning I thought I'd spend some time on the Internet checking out schools with advanced degree programs in social work. If you don't mind my using your computer."

His eyes narrowed, a muscle ticked in his jaw. "No problem."

His agreement contained little understanding and a whole lot of resentment. "I need to do this, Walker. I've relied on other people to do my thinking for me all my life. I have to be able to care for Susie-Q on my own."

"Whatever you say."

"I don't want you to talk me out of—"

"It's your decision, Lizzie. You're a big girl now. You can make up your own mind about leaving or staying. I wouldn't think of interfering."

Tugging his hat down sharply, he reined the horse around, and rode back toward the herd. Anger was written in his taut shoulders and rigid length of his spine.

She closed her eyes against the sudden press of tears. How could she make a man as self-confident as Walker understand her need to prove herself competent enough to stand on her own two feet?

She sighed with regret, aware of a slight tenderness between her legs. It had been a long while since she'd made love. But great sex couldn't be the only thing between her and Walker. She wanted him to find her worthy in other ways, too.

She needed to feel worthy in her own right.

He'd given her the freedom to leave or stay, *her decision,* so why was there an empty sensation in the pit of her stomach?

She observed the roundup action for a while longer, then headed back to the ranch house. A cluster of wild-flowers tucked down in a narrow gully attracted her attention. She dismounted to pluck a few before continuing home.

Home. That was a lovely word, almost as lovely as the flowers she'd picked. But she had no home to call her own—not in California and not here in Montana. A temporary housekeeper was all she could claim.

She'd felt just as temporary growing up, never a permanent part of the schools she attended or even a full-time resident of her parents' house. Nowhere had she fully belonged.

Back at the ranch house, the only thing she could find to put the flowers in was a quart mason jar. She poured water into the container, arranged the flowers and placed them in the center of the kitchen table.

For the first time since she'd arrived at the Double O, she felt as though she'd added some small touch of herself to the house. It seemed such a little thing to do.

As soon as she fed Suzanne her midmorning bottle and got her down for a nap, she went into Walker's office. With a mixture of excitement and regret, she sat in front of his computer. A woman needed a career. A life and choices of her own.

Only then would she be free to choose what her heart cried out for her to do.

DIESEL SMOKE PUFFED from the truck's exhaust as the last of the truck-and-trailer rigs filled with Double O cattle pulled away from the corral. Walker's horse heaved a sigh as if he knew the day's work was over. Walker wished he could ease his tension as easily.

He'd set the boys and Speed to work picking up the corral and hauling it back to the main ranch. They were struggling to load the pieces into the back of his stake bed truck.

Mounted on a rangy Appaloosa next to Walker, Eric hooked his knee over the saddle horn and relaxed. "If we can keep the rest of the herd intact, the year won't be a total loss."

At the moment, the herd was the least of Walker's problems. *Lizzie was going to leave him.* He could have been gored by a bull and it wouldn't have hurt as much.

"We need rain," he said, his voice gravelly and his throat as dry as the landscape.

Eric eyed him from beneath the rim of his Stetson. "What you need is some cheering up. Ever since Lizzie rode off this morning, you've been as glum as a porcupine with his quills plucked. Seems to me if I had a woman like her waiting at home for me—"

"She's leaving."

His head jerked up. "Today?"

"Soon, I'd guess. She's decided to go back to college."

"That's an admirable goal but I thought you two—"

"We're not."

Eric thumbed his hat back. "You don't seem too happy about her decision."

"None of my business."

"You could make it your business. Unless she's already married."

"She's not." Walker nailed his brother with a look that was meant to shut him up, although it had never worked before. "You seem to think I'm some kind of a ladies' man. Well, you and Rory ended up with all of that talent in the family."

"If she's not leaving right away you've got time to change her mind. If that's what you want."

What he wanted was Lizzie. In his life. In his bed. Forever. He'd thought last night that his dream was within his grasp, that Lizzie would be his. No woman could enjoy lovemaking as much as she had and then simply walk away. He'd been so damn sure!

But that's what she'd done this morning, announcing she was going back to school. She'd walked away.

He'd promised not to interfere.

Some great shakes he was at courting a woman!

"Maybe she just hasn't figured out Grass Valley is a terrific place to live."

"She's a city slicker, man. You expect her to enjoy a place like this? First thing she did when she got here was ask if there was a deli in town that delivers."

"That's probably because she's never been to a rodeo." He grinned like a cocky fool. "Girls can't resist a rodeo cowboy. You should have given it a try."

"I like my body held together the old-fashioned way, not with metal pins and Super Glue."

Shrugging as though the rodeo business hadn't nearly killed him, Eric said, "Makes for a little excitement when I go through the metal detectors at the airport."

Walker glanced away. He remembered the day Eric had been stomped by a two-ton Brahma bull. He hurt then for his brother; he hurt now for himself.

"Come on," he said. "Let's get the rest of the corral fence down and into the truck. I don't want to stay out here all night."

In spite of what she'd said, Walker wanted to get back to Lizzie. Maybe she hadn't found a school she wanted to attend. Maybe her grades weren't good enough.

Maybe she'd had second thoughts.

Swearing under his breath at the futility of his dreams, he reined his horse around. What chance did he have with a woman as smart and sophisticated as Lizzie? A woman who had twice planned to marry men with megabucks?

Unless, as Eric suggested, there was still time to get her to fall in love with a rodeo cowboy who'd never lasted his full eight seconds on a bronc.

"DID YOU SEE ME LASSO that ol' cow? Did yah?" Frankie's excitement about the day's roundup bubbled over at the dinner table, making him forget to eat his hamburger as he recounted his heroics.

"It was a yearling, you jerk face," Fridge said. He popped the final bite of his second hamburger in his mouth.

"And you fell off your horse trying to get the rope around the poor guy's neck," Bean Pole said, giving him a poke with his elbow.

"Well, I got him, didn't I?"

Speed nodded his approval. "You did fine, Chicago. Just fine. We'll make a cowboy of you yet."

The boy beamed at Speed's praise.

Toying with the small helping of barbecue beans she'd served herself, Elizabeth repressed a smile. She noticed Walker was unusually subdued. He hadn't met her gaze since he'd come in for dinner and hadn't said a word except in response to a direct question, not participating in the animated conversation around the table.

Her fault, she realized. She'd upset him by telling him her plans. Surely he could respect her need to be her own person before she relied again on someone else.

Suzanne started to fuss in her car seat. Before Elizabeth reacted, Scotty was on his feet.

"You finish your dinner, honey," Elizabeth said. "I'll get her."

"I'm all done." Unbuckling the baby's safety strap, he lifted Suzanne into his arms. "Besides, she likes me to play with her."

"She does indeed," Elizabeth agreed. "You make a wonderful big brother."

Quieting instantly, Suzanne gazed with happy devotion at the young savior who'd rescued her from the confines of her chair. "Yeah. My mom said that, too, until her new boyfriend got tired of me hanging around."

How any woman could desert her own son was beyond Elizabeth's understanding. And to do that to a child as sensitive as Scotty brought a dreadful lump to her throat. Of all the boys in Walker's care, Scotty was the easiest to love. If he belonged to her, Elizabeth probably would have smothered him with hugs. As it was, there were times when she couldn't resist mussing his red hair or giving his shoulders a quick squeeze.

Finished with dinner, Bean Pole and Fridge shoved back from the table and began clearing their plates.

"You boys worked hard today," Elizabeth said. "As long as Scotty has everything under control with Susie-Q, I'll take care of the dishes. You can relax and watch TV."

The youngsters checked with Speed for his approval.

Walker spoke first. "You guys go on. I'll handle the kitchen duties tonight."

Surprised, Elizabeth shot him a questioning look. He didn't look in her direction.

With a reprieve from evening chores, the boys wasted no time lingering in the kitchen. Neither did Speed, which left Elizabeth alone with Walker.

She stacked plates to carry to the counter. "You get the cows safely off to the meat packer?"

"Yep."

He brushed past her with the plate of extra buns, their arms grazing each other. The heat of sexual awareness shot down hers along with memories of their night together. She drew in a quick breath.

"You find out what you needed about colleges?"

With an effort, she blanked out the vivid images that had popped into her head. "A lot of California schools offer what I'm looking for, including U.C. Berkeley, which is right across the bay from where I grew up.''

He scooped up the unused silverware from the table and put them back in the drawer. ''You thinking about moving back home then?''

''With my parents? No, it would be better if I'm on my own with Susie-Q.''

Without acknowledging her statement, he began scraping the remnants of dinner from the dirty plates into the sink.

''It's important that I learn to be independent,'' she added. ''I won't be a good role model for Susie-Q if I'm forever relying on someone else.'' Including the cowboy who'd stolen her heart.

He flipped on the garbage disposal, effectively silencing any further conversation.

Reaching past him, she switched it off. ''Walker, I know you're mad at me but unless you try to understand—''

''You're leaving. It's no big deal. You ran away from that other guy. It makes sense you'd—''

''I didn't *run* away, exactly. I just didn't know how to stand up for myself. It's something I need to learn.'' Those lessons, she suspected, were going to be painful.

Turning, he leveled her a hard-eyed look. ''Have you ever been to a rodeo?''

She blinked at the quick change of topic, mentally trying to imagine where he was going with his question. ''No, I haven't.''

''Before you leave Montana, you ought to see one.''

Was he asking her out? Or hurrying her on her way?

"I suppose that would be a good idea," she said hesitantly. "If I have the chance."

"There's one in Havre this weekend. I'll take you." He flicked on the disposal again. "We'll be gone all day. Scotty will take care of Susie-Q for you. By the way, the flowers on the table are a nice touch."

Stunned, she simply stared openmouthed at Walker, her mind reeling. He'd noticed the flowers and given her the least romantic invitation she'd ever received from a man.

But one she didn't consider refusing, not when it meant she'd be able to spend an entire day with Walker.

Before she left the Double O for an independent life her head said she ought to have and her heart didn't want.

Chapter Eleven

Elizabeth's heart felt light as they cruised along the highway toward Havre Saturday morning. There was something invigorating about the warm wind blowing in her face from the open window and sitting next to a hunky cowboy with long legs encased in tight-fitting jeans. It left her feeling breathless as though she were on the verge of hyperventilating.

The rolling landscape slipped by outside the pickup, acres of grassland yellowing from the summer heat with only an occasional tree to punctuate the view of grazing cattle. The ripe scent of sage filled the truck cab without canceling out the masculine aroma of Walker's spicy aftershave.

But somewhere within these pleasurable impressions her arms felt empty. This was the first time since Suzanne's birth that Elizabeth would be away from her baby for any length of time—a whole day. Lord knows how she would have survived going off on a two-week honeymoon without the baby.

"I miss Susie-Q," she said.

Glancing in her direction, Walker smiled. His arm

rested comfortably on the windowsill, his big, callused hands guiding the truck with ease—just as he'd guided her with the same confidence to sexual pleasure when they'd made love. With little effort she could recall the feel of those hands caressing her. Loving her.

Battling her heated reaction to the images that popped into her head, she forced her gaze back outside.

"Everyone needs a day off now and then," he said.

"I know. But I'm not sure Scotty is old enough to handle a baby for an entire day on his own."

"Speed's there with him. He won't let anything go wrong."

Glancing back at Walker, her gaze collided with his dark, sympathetic eyes. "I left the doctor's phone number on the counter. And my cell phone number."

He lifted his brows. "You turned your phone on?"

"In case of an emergency."

"Slick, your baby will be just fine. You need to concentrate on enjoying the moment."

She nodded. "You're right." There might not be many more of these moments when she'd have Walker all to herself. She desperately wanted to etch every nuance in her memory, every sigh, every scent, every touch, so she could call them up when loneliness overtook her, as she was sure it would after she left the Double O.

She drew a deep breath, cataloging the myriad aromas in the air.

"So tell me about this grand rodeo we're about to see."

"Not so grand. Havre is bigger than Grass Valley but not by much."

He proceeded to wax on about bronc and bull riding, calf roping and barrel racing, events Elizabeth might have glimpsed on TV but had never seen in person. Her apprehension about being gone so long from Suzanne was slowly replaced with excitement over a new adventure.

A rodeo! Not exactly the equestrian events she was used to but ones that felt exactly right for this wide-open country filled with independent men and women willing to challenge a horse, a bull or the land to prove themselves.

She envied their grit and determination.

"And then after the rodeo," he continued, "we'll stop by the local bordello."

"We'll what?" she gasped.

His lips hitched into a grin. "For supper. The bordello has been restored with more, uh, acceptable activities. It's a great place to eat."

Laughing, Elizabeth landed a mock punch on his arm, and tried to ignore a sense of regret that the bordello didn't still serve its original purpose...and that she wasn't the woman waiting for Walker to walk her upstairs to her room.

WALKER WHEELED HIS TRUCK into a row of similar pickups in the makeshift parking lot outside the rodeo arena. Dust billowed into the air, shifting downward to settle yet another layer of dirt on nearby vehicles.

He popped the cab door open, got out and went

around to the passenger side of the truck. He held up his arms to help Lizzie out. Not that she couldn't make it on her own. He just wanted a chance to touch her again.

Resting her hands on his shoulders, she looked down at him with her sky-blue eyes, a smile playing at the corners of her lips. "And so begins our new adventure."

"Well, shoot, Slick, if I'd known you were looking for adventure, I'd have pulled into Helmet's Motel down the street," he drawled. "Talk about an adventure!"

"Oh, you!"

Her eyes sparkled and a flush stole into her cheeks as he lifted her down, his hands lingering a little too long at her waist. She felt so good to hold, yet his grasp was tenuous at best.

She'd be leaving soon. The pain of knowing that twisted a knot in his gut.

Slinging his arm casually over her shoulders, he walked them toward the ticket booth wrapped with red, white and blue bunting for the Fourth of July celebration. Colorful banners hung limply over the tops of stands waiting for a breeze to catch them and flutter them patriotically.

Inside the arena a cheer went up for a junior-division performer finishing his event. In the parking lot, men with meaty, tattooed arms swilled beer from cans while sitting on truck tailgates. Curvaceous women in their teens and twenties strutted their stuff in snakeskin boots and skintight pants hoping to attract the attention of a rodeo cowboy—groupies interested in a good time and not particular with whom they partied.

Walker couldn't imagine Lizzie being a part of the rodeo scene. It wasn't her style. Too far from her ritzy San Francisco upbringing.

Her designer jeans were classier than those worn by the groupies, her cropped top baring a band of flesh at her midriff when she moved just right, soft skin his fingers itched to touch again. She'd slung a purse over her shoulder—a real leather purse no doubt from some upscale boutique. Only the ratty straw hat perched on her head made her look like she might belong at a rodeo, and that wasn't a part of her regular wardrobe but a loan from Walker. He had to be crazy to think she'd want to fit in with his world.

He stopped at the ticket booth and paid for seats near the judges' stand.

"You want something to eat before we go in? Hot dogs. Hamburgers. Coffee. Beer."

"It's a little early for lunch. Coffee would be fine for me and maybe one of those big pretzels."

He grinned. "Good choice. One of my favorites." It was a weak attempt, but he was determined to point out everything they had in common no matter how minor. Sure, he'd promised he wouldn't interfere with her decision. But that didn't mean he couldn't nudge it in his direction when he had a chance.

Coffee and soft pretzels in hand, they made their way into the stands and found their seats. A couple of

Grass Valley families were there. Walker said hello and introduced Lizzie.

"Are you going to ride today?" Chuck Beaverton, a middle-aged rancher from south of town, asked. His wife and two of his children were seated with him.

"I gave that up years ago after a bronc dropped me on the back of my skull one too many times."

"Our Amy is in the barrel racing contest. And Josh, here, took second in the calf roping in his division." He gave his son an affectionate pat on the back, which made the ten-year-old blush.

"Good job, Josh," Walker said. "We'll be sure to root for Amy, too."

Although the grandstand was partially covered to provide shade, Elizabeth still found herself squinting in the bright sunlight. Dust hung in the air and coated her skin like fine powder. Despite all of that, there was an electricity in the air and a sense of comraderie, almost as if everyone there was part of the same family.

Except Elizabeth.

She sat down as yet another man down the row called to Walker. Shouting over the sound of the loud-speaker blaring music between events, Walker and his friend talked about the drought and the lowering water level of the Sage River, then Walker sat down beside her on the hard bench. His heat radiated through two layers of denim to warm more than her leg.

"Do you know everyone here?" she asked, scooting over to make room for him. Their thighs brushed together, his hard and muscular.

"Probably not everyone but a fair number, I'd guess. That's what happens when you stay in the place where you grew up."

Elizabeth couldn't begin to know everyone in Marin County, not to mention San Francisco. But the country club was a tight-knit community unto itself. There were leaders and followers and those who didn't quite fit in. Given her family's wealth, the Tildens were among the leaders. She suspected in Grass Valley, and here in Havre, men and women were judged for themselves, not the size of their bank accounts.

From the way people treated Walker, it was obvious he was well respected in the community. Elizabeth wasn't so sure she'd stack up as well. She had so little to contribute to a town like this, or any town, she thought grimly.

But she was going to change that. She'd get her master's degree. Learn to help kids.

She slanted Walker a look. She'd also lose the man she loved in the process of pursuing her need to be self-reliant. It didn't seem like a fair trade.

With a few static pops coming from the loudspeaker, the announcer introduced the first contender in the barrel race.

The young woman tugged her Stetson down firmly on her head and bent over her cow pony's neck, waiting for the starting gun to sound.

At the crack of the pistol, she dug her heels into the horse's flanks, racing toward two barrels set about thirty paces apart. Within seconds she rounded the far one, the horse's hooves throwing up big clods of dirt and headed back at full speed toward the starting line.

In spite of herself, Elizabeth caught the excitement, stood and cheered for the stranger as her time was announced.

"That was great!" she cried amid an unenthusiastic ripple of applause.

"Actually her time was slow," Walker commented. "She took the turn too wide and the horse almost lost his legs."

"Well, it looked pretty good to me."

But as the event progressed, Elizabeth realized Walker was right. The more skilled riders skimmed by the far barrel with barely a breath of air between horse and obstacle, and their speed in the straight away had the horses' muscles flexing powerfully.

Amy Beaverton took second place in the event, tying her brother's efforts. The young woman's family cheered loudly when she accepted the red ribbon and pinned it to her horse's bridle.

"You know, I bet I could do pretty well at barrel racing," Elizabeth said as the winners took a celebratory lap around the arena.

"I don't think they'd let you use an English saddle."

"I can ride Western." She lifted her chin defensively. "I've been riding with a Western saddle for almost a month now."

"And jumping my horses whenever it takes your fancy," he teased.

"I haven't fallen off yet, have I?" Which was more

than she could say about Frankie, who'd taken a tumble yesterday when he hadn't cinched his saddle properly.

"Only because Tillamook would be embarrassed if his rider went head over teakettle."

She elbowed him in the ribs. She loved the way he teased her, though she wasn't about to let him know that. Her family was too serious. Overly concerned about appearances, they missed opportunities to simply have a good time. Walker, despite his conservative nature, knew how to laugh.

She liked that about him—among his many other admirable attributes.

As the sun rose to its zenith, the air grew warmer, and sweat edged down between her breasts and dampened her face. She decided it was time to take advantage of a lull in the action. "I think I could use that beer you mentioned."

"You got it. Want to come with me?"

She shrugged. "Sure."

The crowd jostled them, bumping them one against the other, his arm protectively around her shoulders. She noticed more than one woman eyeing Walker with open interest. It would be that way anywhere Walker went—women drawn to his rugged masculinity. His sense of presence. His stark virility. His huge heart and his stern yet gentle manner with kids.

She wondered again that he'd never married, that his high school sweetheart had chosen someone else and he'd never found another woman to love. His house cried out for a large family, babies and children filling all those bedrooms. And boys like Scotty and Frankie, Bean Pole and Fridge, who needed an extra dose of love.

A lump formed in her throat, and she washed it down with her first sip of beer. The bitter taste lingered on her tongue. The woman he married would have to be as strong and steady as Walker himself. Nothing less would do.

"Ladies and gentlemen," the announcer shouted over the loudspeaker as Walker and Elizabeth made their way back to their seats. "We're about to begin the open competition for the calf roping contest. We need all the entrants to take their places behind the shoot."

Elizabeth checked the holding pin where a dozen calves had been corralled. The poor little creatures looked frightened, their eyes wide.

"I'm not sure I'm going to like this event," she said.

"Why not? The riders don't get hurt and neither do the calves."

"No? How would you like to be chased by eight hundred pounds of horseflesh?"

He chuckled. Taking her hand, he threaded his fingers through hers. "Now, don't you go rooting for the calf. That'll get you thrown out of the county."

"Somebody has to root for the underdog."

The gate went up on the chute, someone prodded the calf into hurried flight. A second later the two riders—one with a rope and the other there to herd the animal into the roper's path—got their go ahead and shot out after the calf.

"Come on, honey!" Elizabeth shouted. "Run for your life!"

The frightened calf made it three-quarters of the length of the arena before a rope circled his neck like a noose. In the same moment, the rider dismounted in one fluid motion, wrestled the bawling calf to the ground and looped another rope around the animal's legs. The man held up his hands in victory.

With the crowd cheering, Elizabeth shot Walker a dismayed look. "Darn! The cowboy won!"

Their eyes met and held.

"Cowboys don't always win, Slick. It's not in the cards."

A shiver of regret slid down her spin. *City slickers didn't always come out on top, either.*

THE BORDELLO HAD BEEN turned into a small, two-story hotel with dark wood siding and lacy curtains in the windows. Inside, the first floor boasted a lounge and dining room. A huge mirror etched with the outline of a voluptuous, naked woman hung behind the mahogany bar and garish red-flocked wallpaper provided a backdrop for the small tables crowded into the remaining floor space. The ripe scents of cigarette smoke, stale beer, sizzling beef and warm bodies filled the air.

A good portion of the post-rodeo crowd was squeezed into every available space. To move around the room, Elizabeth had to plaster herself against

Walker, letting him act as a battering ram to make their way through the densely packed revelers. Not that she objected overly much to having her arms wrapped around his midsection.

He actually found them a table, shoving his way in just as the former occupants stood to leave. A nearby cowboy who'd been waiting started to object but abruptly stopped when Walker gave him the evil eye.

"This is great, isn't it?" he shouted over the noise and confusion once they were seated.

"Wonderful. Very intimate." Indeed, their shoulders were knocking together. No doubt they could have a private conversation and no one—including each other—would be able to hear a word. And how a waitress would ever get to them through the mob to take their orders was beyond Elizabeth. "Is it always this busy?"

"Only during rodeo weekends. The rest of the time it's pretty quiet."

Elizabeth wondered if they shouldn't come back another day then, a day when the restaurant wasn't so crowded.

He handed her a one-page menu spattered with all manner of stains. "The prime rib is good. I like the T-bone myself."

Man food, she mused. Then again, he'd put up with her inept efforts at cooking for a month. He deserved a reward. "I'll try the prime rib." Despite Walker's rave reviews of the place, she expected the meat to be tough and gristly.

Once again she was proved wrong. Somehow

Walker managed to place their meal orders and get them a pitcher of beer with two glasses. As nearly as she could tell he'd used hand signals to order from the buxom-blond waitress, who finally made her way through the crowd to deliver their dinners.

Her first bite of prime rib nearly melted in her mouth. "This is delicious." Fully as tasty as anything she'd enjoyed at the finest restaurants in San Francisco.

"You're in cattle country, honey." He sliced off a bite of steak, popped it in his mouth and chewed with obvious enjoyment. "We pride ourselves on serving the best beef in the country, no matter what the wags say about Chicago or Omaha."

"You've got me convinced." Discovering a day of fresh air and excitement had given her an appetite, Elizabeth dug into her meal, relishing every bite.

The crowd swirled around them, occasionally bumping their table as the patrons shifted positions like a swarm of ants climbing over an anthill. Recorded country music blared over the loudspeakers. People shouted to be heard yet their voices were strangely muted in the general cacophony.

For the most part, Elizabeth was aware only of Walker—the way he held his knife and fork, the flex of his jaw when he chewed, a tiny fleck of garlic bread that was caught on his upper lip in exactly the spot she'd like to kiss. When he licked his lips, banishing the crumb, her womb clenched.

He sipped his beer, his Adam's apple bobbing in the tanned column of his throat, and she tasted the tangy beer on her tongue mixed with the sweeter flavor of his skin.

Sitting shoulder to shoulder, the sleeve of his blue chambray shirt brushed against her arm each time he raised his fork or lowered it. Hidden beneath the table, their thighs touched, and heat flowed through her body like a molten river.

She'd never imagined eating dinner with a man could be such a sensual experience. So carnal she could barely catch her breath.

But Walker was no ordinary man.

He was the man she loved.

To her surprise, about the time they finished dinner someone removed the tables from a minuscule dance floor at one end of the lounge area and a three-piece band appeared—drums, base fiddle and saxophone. The mustached musicians wore cowboy hats, blue-stripped shirts, jeans and well-worn boots, an appropriate uniform for the country-western music they played.

"You want to risk your toes?" Walker tilted his head toward the dance floor.

She wanted to risk far more than her toes but for Walker's sake she didn't dare. For now, to be held in his arms would have to be enough.

With a nod, she slipped the strap of her purse over her shoulder, shoved back her chair and stood. "Before we're through, you may be glad you wear cowboy boots. I'm a little out of practice."

"I'm betting you had lessons at those fancy boarding schools you attended."

"Ballet, ballroom and even Irish step dancing, which doesn't mean I'm not capable of doing a fair amount of damage to a man's toes when I set my mind to it."

His lips canted into a half smile. "I plan to keep your mind occupied on things other than my feet." His husky words sounded like a promise.

With his hand at her midriff, he ushered her through the maze of tables and chairs onto the dance floor. Smoke drifted like clouds through columns of light cast by red and blue floodlights.

Stopping at the edge of the dance floor, he pulled her around and took her in his arms. Her head rested naturally on his shoulder; her body curved into his. Closing his hand around hers, he brought her fingers to his lips.

Despite the press of bodies all around them, she shivered when he kissed her fingertips.

"I miss seeing your nails polished."

"Fancy nails aren't very practical for working around the house."

"I know." Regret hummed in his voice in counterpoint to the lonesome melody played by the saxophone.

She needn't have worried about remembering her dancing lessons. There was little room to move and barely enough to breathe. When she did inhale it was Walker's spicy aftershave that tickled her nostrils along with his muskier scent, one that was all male.

They rocked to the music rather than danced. Walker's broad hand rested at the small of her back.

Warming her flesh between her jeans and cropped top. Enticing her.

When he tugged her more fully into the nest of his hips, the ridge of his arousal pressed against her abdomen. Tempting her.

Closing her eyes, she let the world of tactile sensations overcome her and found herself mesmerized by the sweep of lights across her eyelids. Red and blue blended in a kaleidoscope of color, turning the images in her mind indigo.

She pictured them dancing, Walker so tall and broad shouldered that he dwarfed her. Without a single word of objection, she fell under his spell, moving as he moved. Swaying to a beat that had little to do with the rhythm the band was playing and everything to do with the heavy pulse that thudded in her heart.

For years, she'd meekly allowed her family to press her to follow *their* goals, not hers. Now she needed to be strong. To be her own person. Ironically Walker, the image of self-confidence, by providing a refuge had helped her to see the path to independence.

But how would she find the strength to leave him?

Or the courage to remain?

Walker nuzzled his lips next to her ear. "Lizzie, honey, I want to take you upstairs."

"Upstairs?" she said dreamily.

"I reserved us a room, in case we wanted to spend the night."

She lifted her head and looked into his eyes. His need was there as well as a reflection of her own.

"Getting a little sure of yourself, cowboy?"

"Anyone who raises cattle has to be an optimist."

"What about the baby? Scotty didn't volunteer for the night shift."

"I warned Speed we might be delayed. He'll stay at the ranch house with Susie-Q. And if there's an emergency, he'll still be able to reach you on your cell phone."

A whole night with Walker. No fear of discovery or the baby interrupting them. Selfishly she knew she wouldn't refuse. Couldn't refuse.

Her throat closed down tight, her whispered "Yes" barely audible.

She hadn't noticed the stairway before, the elaborately carved walnut banister, the worn oak steps that had felt the weight of thousands of men and women mounting them for this same purpose. To ease the ache of loneliness. To share the ultimate intimacy for one moment in time.

To love one another.

Upstairs the music was muted but the beat continued to throb through the floor. She felt it pulsate on the soles of her feet and move upward until it drummed at the very core of her being.

A four-poster mahogany bed draped in red velvet greeted them in their room. On the matching vanity, colorful glass bottles of perfume in turn-of-the-century style and pots of makeup lay scattered about as though the room's occupant had just finished preparing for her evening's work. A modesty screen sat in one corner of the room, a filmy negligee tossed carelessly over the top.

"Looks like we're appealing to a man's fantasy," she said.

Tipping her chin up, he brushed a soft kiss to her lips. "Are you telling me it isn't your fantasy, too?"

She shivered at the delectable thought. What woman wouldn't want to be free to dispense her favors without remorse or morning-after regrets?

"Does that mean I should seduce you?"

Framing her face with his big hands, he kissed her again, lingering longer this time. "I'd be a willing accomplice but you may have to hurry. I'm already three-quarters gone under your spell."

She laughed a low, throaty sound. "That makes two of us. We'd better not waste any time."

The subtleties of seduction forgotten, Walker claimed her mouth in a deep, possessive kiss while his clever hands made short work of the buttons on her blouse. Despite her shaking fingers, she returned the favor, ridding him of his shirt as she toed off her boots. She moaned into his mouth as he snatched her bra away and covered her breasts with his hands, squeezing and kneading them.

She fumbled with the snap on his jeans, finally shoving his pants below his hips and releasing the hard pulsing length of him to cradle in her palms.

Before she could catch her breath, he'd tugged her jeans down around her ankles, then all the way off. He backed her up against one of the decorative bedposts, lifted her and thrust himself into her. She cried out in surprise, marveled at his strength, then wrapped her legs around his waist. He drove himself into her again and again, holding her suspended, and felt herself come apart in his arms.

Limply she clung to him. "Oh, my..."

"What were you saying about seduction?"

"My skills are definitely rusty. I'll have to try again...in a minute." As soon as the room stopped spinning and she regained her ability to breathe.

Walker laid her on top of the big feather bed, removing the rest of her clothes and dropping his own to the floor. This was the night he wanted Lizzie to remember wherever she might be, Montana, California, anywhere in the world. When she thought of him he wanted his taste on her tongue, the feel of his hands still etched in her memory, the sense of him filling her as no man ever could again.

With every bit of self-control he could muster, he set about doing just that. Putting his mark on her. Possessing her. Creating memories that would never be forgotten no matter how long they both might live. He'd always be a part of her...and she a part of him.

Finally he reached his limit. He could no longer endure the sweet torture of denying himself. With his last bit of reason, he rolled on a condom then placed himself between her legs.

"Look at me, Lizzie. I want you to know who's loving you."

"I do."

Her eyes widened as he entered her, her slick welcome easing his access, and he began to rock within her. His eyes never left hers nor did she look away. The faster he moved the more rapidly her breasts rose and fell. Never missing a beat, he cupped her breasts. His thumbs worked her nipples until they were as rigid as his own body.

Sobbing, she grasped the sheets at her side, her legs pulling him deeper and deeper inside her.

With a final thrust, he gave himself up to the sensation of being one with his Lizzie. For tonight.

Hoping it would be forever.

ELIZABETH ROUSED FROM HER dreamy stupor to find Walker sprawled next to her on the bed, snoring softly. She smiled, and in the light cast by the bed lamp gave herself over to the pleasure of examining his beautiful masculine body.

A light smattering of saddle-brown hair covered his chest, arrowing down his flat belly toward the nest where his penis was now at rest. Unable to resist, she ran her hand over the uneven scar on his thigh. His adolescent battle wound from showing off with a rifle.

Tenderly she brushed her lips to his scar.

"I hope you know you're starting something I plan to finish," he said.

Noting his rapidly recovering arousal, she smiled at him. "What if I plan to take matters into my own… hands?"

"I'd be hard-pressed to object."

"I thought as much."

He groaned as she cupped him and her lips intimately caressed him. Excitement pulsed through her at his visible response. She dallied with her tongue, driving herself crazy. He rewarded her with a fierce growl that came from deep in his lungs as he pulled her up to straddle him.

Downstairs, the music continued to pulse. But their beat went faster. Harder. Until she cried out again.

While she was still limp with exhaustion, he reversed their positions and drove into her once more, sending her beyond the brink.

THE NEXT TIME ELIZABETH woke she had no idea what time it was. Or what the heavy weight was that rested across her chest. But she was vaguely aware of a delicious tenderness between her legs—and an annoying ringing in her ears.

She lifted her head and squinted at the bright light that flooded through the lacy curtains. The bordello bedroom was a sight to behold with clothes strewn everywhere. As memories rushed back to her, she knew no lady-of-the-evening had enjoyed her time more in this bed than Elizabeth had. She assumed, with her partner splayed half on top of her, that Walker had had a pleasant evening as well.

Which didn't explain that dreadful ringing sound.

Who on earth would be calling her—

Despite the weight of Walker's arm across her, she bolted from the bed. Her first thought was of Suzanne. A crisis. Shards of panic ripped through her. And guilt for having stolen a night with Walker.

Frantically she dug into her purse and pulled out her cell phone.

"Yes. What's happened?"

"Susie-Q's just fine, Miss Lizzie," Speed said. "It's the boys I'm worried about."

She did a mental double-take. "The boys?" What on earth—

Walker grabbed for the phone but she didn't let go. Instead she pressed her head to his and they both listened.

"All four of 'em are gone, Miss Lizzie. Sometime in the night they just up and left."

"They ran away?" Walker asked.

"Their clothes 'n' stuff are still here, boss, like they was planning to come back. Don't know what got into their heads." He sounded more perplexed than worried.

"Maybe they simply decided to sleep outside last night," she suggested. "It was warm. They could have ridden the horses to the river, or maybe into town."

"Nope. The horses are all still here. I checked."

"Did they just walk off? Hitch a ride? Maybe a friend—"

"Thing is, Miss Lizzie, they took your car. Just drove it away in the night and I didn't even hear 'em leave."

She looked at Walker and saw her own shock and fear reflected in his dark eyes.

"Stay put, Speed." Slipping the phone from her fear-numbed fingers, Walker swung his legs around and stood beside the rumpled bed. "We'll be there as soon as we can."

Chapter Twelve

Walker ignored the speed limits on the highway and broke every damn one of them setting a record getting back to the ranch.

Sitting beside him, Lizzie was as pale as a china doll, her hands locked together in her lap. She'd barely taken time to dress and brush her hair, twisting it on top of her head, fastening the blond strands in place with one of the bordello's ballpoint pens with a red cap. She'd tossed her straw hat on the jump seat behind her.

"I'll never forgive myself if any of the boys are hurt," she said.

"Yeah. I know how you feel. And if the boys aren't hurt when I find them, they'll damn well be hurting when I'm done with them."

Reaching across the truck, she rested her hand on his thigh. "Something terrible must have happened to make all four of them go off with my car. They love you. They know you'd be upset."

"Kids sometimes do strange things." Or they could be led into trouble. At the moment, he suspected

Frankie might be at the bottom of this stunt. That kid was still too raw, too unsettled to be trusted. He should have known to keep a closer eye on the boy.

"Maybe if we hadn't stayed away overnight," she whispered, her voice choked.

He covered her hand with his. "No guilt. No regrets. You can't predict what a kid is going to do, particularly youngsters that have been in the system for a while." From his own experience in foster care, he knew that to be true. He'd run away or gotten into trouble so many times he couldn't even count them— until he landed at the Double O and Oliver Oakes took him in hand. He wished he'd done as well for the boys.

Dust billowed up behind his pickup as he whipped the truck from the highway onto the dirt ranch road. Moments later the house came into view, Eric's police cruiser parked out in front. Noticeably missing was Lizzie's silver-blue BMW.

"Why are the police here?" Lizzie gasped.

"It's Eric's cruiser. I called him while you were in the bathroom. I figured he'd be some help finding the boys. *And* your car."

She nodded. "Of course. You're right. But I don't plan to press charges about my car."

"Let's talk about that after we get the kids back where they belong." And find out why the hell they decided to take a joy ride in the middle of the night.

He pulled up in front of the house and Lizzie was out of the truck almost before he stopped. He was only paces behind her by the time she shoved open the front door.

"Have you heard anything about the boys?" she asked, zeroing in on Susie-Q, who was in Speed's arms.

Looking relieved, he handed the baby over to her. "Not a word, Miss Lizzie. I jest cain't think why they'd run off like that, without saying a word to me. Specially Scotty. He was counting on feeding Susie-Q her breakfast this morning."

Walker sent a silent question in Eric's direction.

"I put out an APB on the car," he said. "Nothing yet."

Taking off his Stetson, Walker balanced it on the back of the couch. "We sure didn't see them on the highway coming in from Havre."

"They could have gone west, maybe into Idaho." Looking grim, Eric glanced out the window as if he hoped to catch sight of the boys returning. He'd had his own memories of foster care, none of them any better than Walker's. "I'll expand the search to other states if we don't hear something soon."

"Tell us exactly what happened last night, Speed," Walker asked.

"Well, now, long 'bout ten o'clock young Scotty got a phone call. Didn't think much about it."

"Who from?" Lizzie asked.

The foreman shrugged. "A woman, I'd say. She didn't say her name, not to me anyway. Right after that, the boys all went out to the bunkhouse to bed. I went on to bed myself. Used the back bedroom upstairs where I could still hear Miss Susie-Q." He scratched at his gray sideburns as though that might help him remember the details. "When they didn't come in this morning, I went lookin' for 'em. They were gone and so was your car, Miss Lizzie."

Frowning, Elizabeth glanced around the room at the men. She hadn't noticed Scotty with any girls on their trips into town. He was a little too young for the adolescent crowd that hung out at the ice-cream shop. So what woman would be calling him?

"His mother!" she blurted out.

"Whose mother?" Walker asked.

"The only female who'd be calling Scotty would be his mother. Would she know how to find him here?"

Walker shrugged. "I don't know. I don't think social services even knew where his mother had gone off to, and I doubt Mabel would give her the phone number if she turned up."

"Maybe somehow the boy let his mother know where he was," Eric suggested.

"Maybe," Walker conceded.

As Suzanne snuggled in her arms, Elizabeth detected a telltale odor. "I've got to change Susie-Q. Maybe one of you should call his social worker, see if she has any ideas."

Worried sick about the boys, Elizabeth headed upstairs. The only thing that made sense was that Scotty's mother had reached him. But why wouldn't he tell Speed? And why on earth had the other boys gone off with him?

Still puzzling over the problem, she changed Suzanne then carried her into her bedroom. She started to tuck her purse back in the drawer of the end table when she remembered she'd been reluctant to carry her whole stash of cash to a rodeo.

Fearing what she might find—or *not* find—she slowly opened the drawer.

The money was gone!

Someone had taken every single dollar she'd had hidden away—albeit not well hidden.

Frankie seemed the most likely culprit. She'd caught him once looking for money in Walker's office. But he'd been adjusting so well to the ranch, fitting in, feeling good about himself. Or so she'd thought.

And why on earth would all the boys go with him? Surely they had more loyalty to Walker than that.

She felt sick at heart. Betrayed by the boys she'd grown to love. More than anything else, she wanted to know why.

With reluctance, she went downstairs to report what she'd discovered.

Without comment, Eric made a note of the information on the small pad he kept in his shirt pocket.

Walker looked as distressed as she felt that the boys would steal from her.

For the moment there was nothing any of them could do except wait for news.

LATE THAT AFTERNOON, Eric got a call from Great Falls. The police had found four boys and a BMW matching the description in the APB, but no money.

The car had been impounded and the boys locked up in the city jail waiting arraignment on grand theft auto the next morning.

Walker planted his hat on his head. "I'll go get the boys. Probably be back tomorrow."

"I'm going with you," Elizabeth told him.

"They're my responsibility."

"They stole *my* car and *my* money. That makes it my business, too. Besides, Scotty's going to need a woman around."

Walker lowered his brows and glared at her. "You're a stubborn little thing, aren't you?"

She lifted her chin. "You've got that damn straight."

To give Speed a break in the child-care department, Elizabeth called Hetty. The older woman was more than happy to come stay with Suzanne while Elizabeth and Walker went to Great Falls to bring the boys home. Then she packed an overnight case.

Walker did the same.

Unanswered questions weighed down the silence in Walker's truck during the three-hour drive.

The desk sergeant at the police station had no answers for them. Neither did the jail attendant who escorted them through a locked door.

Elizabeth had never visited a jail. The metal bars sent chills down her spine; the pale green paint gave her the creeps, and the oddly antiseptic smell made her want to gag. She had a desperate urge to throw open the windows and let some sunlight inside. And vowed to *never* break so much as a traffic law again.

She couldn't imagine how adolescents might react to the drab yet threatening environment.

Her jaw clenched. These were *her* boys, and she didn't want them locked up for a moment longer than necessary.

She and Walker waited in a dreary interrogation room for the youngsters to be brought in. The scarred table had wobbly legs and so did the chairs surrounding it. Overhead, wire mesh shielded a single glaring lightbulb. The same thick mesh guarded the one window, which was painted over and appeared to have last been opened in some prior century. If this scene didn't scare the boys straight, Elizabeth didn't know what would.

Frankie swaggered in first followed by the rest of the boys.

"Sit down," the guard ordered. "Keep your hands to yourselves. No hugging. No touching. No passing of notes or food. If there's trouble—" he glanced at Walker "—pound on the door or yell."

"Thank you," Walker said with a far calmer demeanor than Elizabeth could have managed. Maybe he'd been here before, or somewhere much like this.

She and Walker sat opposite the boys, who'd yet to meet their eyes.

"You want to tell us what happened?" Walker asked quietly despite the muscle that jerked in his jaw.

Frankie shrugged. "Hey, we wanted to go for a ride. You got some neat wheels, sweetheart. Thanks a—"

Walker slammed his palm down hard on the table,

startling everyone. "A joy ride, is that what this is all about?"

Before any of the boys answered, Elizabeth asked, "Did you take my money, Frankie?"

"Sure, why not? These guys are so out of it, they didn't even know I snitched a few bucks. Figured you wouldn't even notice."

Bean Pole leaned forward. "Hey, wait a minute. You can't take all the blame—"

"Shut up. I did it and I'll take the heat. Nobody has to—"

"It's my fault," Scotty said softly.

Frankie groaned. "Come on, kid. I can do the time. Ain't no big deal."

Elizabeth, despite the guard's orders, reached across the table to take Frankie's hand. "You did it for Scotty, didn't you? The money and the car."

He blustered a little but couldn't meet her eyes. "It's on me, okay? These jerks don't know nothin'. They just wanna go back to mucking stalls. Whoopee! I got better things to do with my life."

"Right. Like spending it in jail." She could have kissed Frankie because she knew he was covering for all the boys, especially Scotty. "Your mother called you, didn't she?"

Scotty lifted his head, his chin trembling, but he didn't say a word.

"Why did she call, son?" Walker asked.

The boy dropped his gaze again. "She needed someone to bail her out."

Elizabeth felt sick to her stomach. A woman who'd

ask her twelve-year-old son to bail her out of trouble ought to be strung up by her thumbs.

"Here in Great Falls?" Walker persisted.

Scotty shrugged. "She said my sister needed her."

"How did she get the phone number at the ranch?" Walker continued his interrogation.

"I wrote to a friend of hers. I thought maybe some-day she'd want—" His voice cracked. "It was my fault Frankie took the money. I didn't even know—"

"It's okay," Elizabeth assured him.

"If he'd just kept his mouth shut," Frankie muttered.

Fridge elbowed him in the ribs. "Maybe next time you oughta be the one to shut up. No way we should've taken Miss Lizzie's money."

"Or her car," Walker pointed out firmly.

"Where's your mother now?" Elizabeth asked Scotty, ignoring the exchange between the boys and Walker.

"I dunno. We got some guy to pay the bail. Mom came out. She gave me a hug…" Tears sheening his eyes, Scotty looked away. "Then she took off with that guy she's been with."

"Where's your sister?"

"I don't know." His chin trembled. "I didn't see her. She might have been in the car. She's not very big. If they'd asked, I would've taken care of her."

"How old is your sister now?"

"I dunno." He shrugged. "She was about Susie-Q's size when Mom went off—" His voice cracked, his throat working to swallow back his tears. "That was a couple of years ago."

Elizabeth thought her heart might break. These boys, who were so loyal to each other, were all hurting for Scotty's sake, and he was hurting the most. She wanted to take every one of them in her arms—Frankie, with all of his cockiness, included.

"We can't get you out tonight, guys," Walker explained. "Not that you don't deserve to be here. A problem like this, you should've talked to Speed. Or called me or Lizzie, not tried to handle it on your own. You're scheduled for court tomorrow morning but we'll try to see the county attorney first. Get you released to us. Unless you'd rather wait it out in jail."

Bean Pole shook his head. "Whatever you say, boss."

Looking frightened, Fridge nodded his agreement. "Are they gonna feed us dinner?"

"I'll see that they do," Walker said.

The other two boys didn't comment.

LEAVING THE JAIL, WALKER drove to a nearby motel, not exactly as classy as Lizzie might be used to but he was too tired to drive around town looking for a vacancy.

"One room or two?" he asked her before getting out of the truck.

"One, unless you'd rather—"

"One's fine by me." He wanted to hold her in his arms, bury his head in the sweet smell of her hair. Somehow he'd failed the boys who'd been put in his care. And, like Scotty, every woman who'd mattered to him had walked away.

Why the hell had he promised not to stop her?

He got the key. The room was on the first floor. When he opened the door, he nearly slammed it shut again. She stepped inside before he could.

"We could go to a nicer place," he said. Institutional was a mild description. Gray walls. A king-size bed with a stained spread. Lamps bolted to the end tables.

"This is fine. Neither one of us is going to get much sleep tonight anyway."

But not for the reason he would have liked, he suspected.

"God, I could kill those kids."

She pressed her finger to his lips. "No, you couldn't. You're too good. Too caring."

"You know you're not going to get a dime of your money back. It's pretty obvious Scotty's mom plans to skip bail."

"The money doesn't matter." She shoved the door shut behind them. "What I don't understand is how *any* woman could entice her son to steal money for her and then walk out on him for the second time. Abandon him again, for God's sake!" Her anger made her voice quiver, her whole body shake.

"It's likely to cost more money tomorrow to bail the boys out. Cash flow is always a problem on a ranch. I'll stop by the bank, see if I can get a loan."

"No, don't do that. It'll be easier if I get the bank

to transfer some funds from my San Francisco account.''

Unable to resist, he cupped her cheek, caressing her smooth skin, as soft as peaches-and-cream ice cream yet as warm as silk. "If you do that, your family will be able to trace you to Great Falls. Finding you from here will be easy.''

"It doesn't matter. It's time I face my family anyway.''

She was ready to get on with the rest of her life. Dread filled his gut and pounded through his veins.

Out of desperation, he pulled her into his arms. For the first time it wasn't a sexual embrace. Something different. Deeper. More urgent and heartfelt.

"Maybe we ought to call it a night, huh?''

She nodded her head against his chest. "I could use a shower.''

"In this place, I can't guarantee the facilities.''

"Wet and warm will be good enough.''

"Alone? Or with a friend?''

She looked up at him, her eyes so full of pain and trouble, he wanted to soothe her almost more than he wanted to love her.

"A girl can always use a friend.''

"Yeah. A guy can, too.''

They took turns lathering each other with the tiny bar of soap the motel provided, shampooed each other's hair. Walker couldn't recall a time when he'd been more intimate with a woman, more a part of her and she a part of him. They dried off together, then slipped into bed. The sheets were coarse, the blanket smelled of disinfectant.

And when they made love, it was sweet and lingering, achingly good in a way Walker had never before imagined. He slept with his arms wrapped around her and tried not to dwell on his urgent need to stop the clock.

THE OFFICIOUS COUNTY attorney, Audry Palmer, wouldn't listen to reason.

"We have a zero tolerance policy for juvenile offenders," she said from behind a desk piled high with files. "It doesn't matter that you don't wish to press charges. The boys stole your car *and* your money. The state of Montana wants them punished."

"I want them home where they belong," Elizabeth said. Where she could give them all the TLC a mother would—or *should,* if she were any kind of decent mother.

"You can be sure the boys will be punished appropriately back at the ranch," Walker assured the woman. "There's no need to lock them up. Two of the boys don't even have a juvenile record."

Ms. Palmer huffed. "They do now."

It took the better part of the day to get through the arraignment, get the BMW from the impound yard and post the bail money. Four subdued boys exited the jail building with their heads down, shoulders slumped and their hands stuffed in their pockets.

Scotty paused on the steps to look around. "I thought maybe my mom..." His voice trailed off.

Instinctively Elizabeth circled his shoulders with her arm and gave him a squeeze. He'd grown in the month she'd been at the ranch. His shoulders a little broader than they had been, his legs longer. He was going to need new jeans before he went back to school. New boots, too, from the looks of his old ones.

Dear heaven, despite how wonderful Walker was with the boys, they needed a mother, too. Someone to worry and fuss over them. A woman strong enough, confident enough to help guide them into the adults they could become.

"I really messed up, didn't I?" Scotty said. "I'm sorry about stealing your car 'n' stuff."

"You love your mother and you did what you thought was best. But now I think you have to worry about yourself."

"What about my sister? She's too little—"

"Come on, you two." Walker cupped his hand around the back of Scotty's neck. "Let's get back to the ranch. There're a lot of stalls needing mucking and fences needing mending."

The three other boys groaned in unison.

"The other guys got in trouble cuz of me," Scotty said. "I'll do whatever needs doing."

"You fellows ever hear of the Three Musketeers?" Walker asked.

Bean Pole lifted his bony shoulders. "Yeah, I guess."

"Well, from now on think of yourselves as the *four* Musketeers. It's one for all and all for one. So let's get on home and see if we've got enough shovels to go around.''

Despite the fact Elizabeth knew she should be getting on with her plans for the future, she couldn't bring herself to take the first step of enrolling for an advanced degree at any of the possible universities she'd found on the Internet. It seemed to her that Scotty—all of the boys, really—were too emotionally fragile to take another loss just now.

And later that evening as she watched the youngsters play with Suzanne so lovingly, Elizabeth knew she couldn't wrench the baby away from them, either. Or leave herself.

Besides, there was their court case to consider, she rationalized. Walker had hired an attorney. She'd have to testify. She couldn't leave. Not yet.

And so she let the next couple of days slip by, postponing her decision. Procrastinating about her own future.

She was baking stuffed pork chops for dinner when she glanced outside. An unfamiliar car had pulled up in front of the house and a man got out, glancing around.

Giving a little cry of recognition, she tossed aside the hot pad she'd had in her hand and ran outside.

Chapter Thirteen

Walker came out of the barn at the sound of a car arriving. He squinted at the unfamiliar vehicle, a non-descript model with Montana plates and a car rental company's license-plate frame.

Puzzled over who would be visiting the Double O in a rental car, he strolled toward the front of the house. Bandit raced out ahead of him, barking for all he was worth at the man who'd climbed out of the driver's side, a city slicker from the way he was dressed in casual pants and an expensive polo shirt that sported a logo where the pocket ought to be.

Walker tensed. The visitor sure as hell didn't look like a door-to-door salesman to him.

Lizzie flew off the front porch calling to the dog. "Down, Bandit. Stay!" Then she ran into the stranger's arms. Lifting her, the man twirled Lizzie around in the air, and they both laughed.

Sitting back on his haunches, Bandit watched the spectacle, his tail wagging tentatively.

In contrast, Walker's first instinct was to get his shotgun and drive the stranger off the Double O and out of the whole damn state. *Nobody* had the right to hold Lizzie that way except *him.*

Nobody had the right to take her away from him.

His hands bunched into fists as he approached, his adrenaline surged and his blood pulsed hot and angry through his veins.

"You want to introduce me to your friend?" he asked tautly. *Before I toss him off my property.*

Lizzie turned, her smile so radiant Walker thought it would rival a summer sunrise. She held out one hand to him but her other arm was still wrapped around the stranger's waist.

"Come here. I want you to meet my brother, Robert Tilden. Robert, this is my, uh, employer, Walker Oakes."

Her *brother?* That drove the steam right out of his fury. His *jealousy,* he mentally corrected. Damn, he'd never been jealous over any woman in his life. Until now. Even at that, he didn't appreciate being referred to as Lizzie's employer. He was a lot more than that to her. At least, after what they'd shared together, he should be.

He extended his hand. "Robert."

Disengaging himself from Lizzie, her brother shook his hand. His grip was firm and his palm wasn't soft, exactly, but he sure as hell didn't have any calluses. Not from the kind of hard work Walker did. Walker would venture the heaviest lift the man did was to put pen to paper and sign a check for whatever he wanted.

"Glad to meet you, Walker. The family's been pretty worried about Elizabeth."

"As you can see, Lizzie's just fine."

Robert cocked a brow at his sister. His hair was a couple of shades darker than hers yet the family resemblance was strong. "*Lizzie?* Is that what you've been calling yourself, Elizabeth?"

Her grin made her look as mischievous as a minx. "I needed a full makeover."

"You know Mother hates nicknames."

"But Mother isn't here, is she?"

Robert laughed. "A new name and a job, too? You've made quite a few changes, I gather."

Elizabeth glanced at Walker. "I've tried." But she wasn't sure it was enough. She didn't know if, despite her weeks here on the ranch, she measured up to what Walker would want in a wife. What he deserved. He'd never said a word about her staying. Granted, he'd promised not to interfere with her plans to go back to school. But he'd had plenty of opportunities to hint— just a little—that he'd be sorry to see her go.

No man ought to be that determined to keep his word.

She hooked her arm through Robert's. "Look, you two, supper's just about ready and I don't want to burn the stuffed pork chops. It's a new recipe I'm trying."

"You *cook?*" her brother gasped.

"I also vacuum, dust, scrub floors and do the laundry," she said smugly.

"And she takes care of Susie-Q," Walker added.

Her brother frowned. "Susie who?"

"Suzanne. Your niece. Walker gives everyone a nickname. He calls me Slick."

"I can hardly wait to hear what name he picks out for me," Robert muttered.

Walker heard him. "You may not like it."

The two men eyed each other with wary distrust. Elizabeth didn't want them fighting. Both Walker and Robert were important to her, and she touched Walker's arm lightly in the hope that he'd recognize her brother's arrival hadn't changed anything between them.

"Walker, while I take Robert inside would you let Speed and the boys know supper's about ready?"

After a heartbeat of hesitation, Walker shrugged. "I'll tell 'em."

Bandit trotted off with Walker and she led Robert into the house. She bent down to pick up the baby clutter leftover from afternoon playtime. Elizabeth might be a housekeeper but she wasn't a very good one. Something about having a baby around left a perpetual mess.

"So you work for Walker, huh?"

She nodded.

"Offhand, I'd say your relationship with him was a lot more than that of employer-employee."

She tried not to blush, which made the heat rush to her cheeks all the more rapidly. "What makes you say that?"

"Sis, that guy is so damn territorial about you, I thought he was going to take off my head before he found out I'm your brother. And after he did find out, it didn't get much better. I'd hate to think what would happen to a man who tried to pick you up in a bar or someplace and Walker was anywhere within a twenty-mile radius.''

At her secret, feminine core, Elizabeth was ashamed of the thrill that shot through her at the prospect of Walker caring that much, wanting her to belong to him that much.

She tried to cover her flare of pleasure by disagreeing with her brother. ''Nonsense. You know men don't try to pick me up.''

''Only because you usually send off don't-touch-me vibes. Otherwise, half the male population of San Francisco would have been out to nail you. I'd say this Walker fellow has made some real progress.''

Heat scalded her cheeks again. She was saved from responding when simultaneously Suzanne announced from upstairs that she was all done with her nap and the dinger on the oven sounded.

''Turn off the oven for me, would you, Robert, while I bring Susie-Q down so you can say hello. You're staying for dinner, aren't you?''

''With you cooking? Is it safe?''

''There's a saloon in town that makes cholesterol-laden hamburgers, if you'd rather.''

He grinned at her, so like the brother she remembered who'd teased her during her growing-up years, at least during those times when they'd both been at home. Despite their frequent separations, she'd always had a soft spot in her heart for her brother. ''I've come a long way to find you. Guess I can take the risk on your cooking.''

As often happened, dinner was a little chaotic. Suzanne needed to be fed at the same time Elizabeth was trying to serve the meal, and Scotty took over by spooning rice mush into her mouth—half of which dribbled out again.

While being helpful, Bean Pole fell over his own feet, spilling a bowl of applesauce all over the floor. Mopping it up resulted in an argument between Bean Pole and Fridge about getting the sticky sauce on Fridge's boots and who would have to polish the boots for church on Sunday.

Elizabeth smiled at the astonished expression on Robert's face as all of the activity went on around him.

She nudged him with her elbow as she sat down at her place next to him. "Home was never like this, was it?"

He chuckled. "Not likely!"

"I love it. I really do." Amazingly she did love everything about this household of mismatched souls who'd somehow turned themselves into a family—the boys who were both emotionally needy and lovingly wholesome despite their best efforts to be juvenile delinquents; Suzanne, who took in all the action with her wide blue eyes; and, Walker, who commanded respect from the head of the table. Yes, she loved it all. Most especially Walker.

Her throat constricted around a bite of pork chop, and for a moment she couldn't breathe. She suspected Robert had come at her mother's behest to take her home—to San Francisco. But *this* was her home, if Walker would only ask her to stay. This was *her* family. Here she could fulfill all of her dreams of helping others, a hands-on social worker to boys who needed her.

If only their foster dad would say he needed her, too.

After dinner, Speed volunteered himself and the boys to clean up the kitchen so she and her brother could visit. Elizabeth couldn't help but be amused when Walker doggedly followed them into the living room.

Sitting on the couch, she jiggled Suzanne on her lap and was rewarded with a grin and a giant drool that landed on her shirt. She wiped at the mess halfheartedly, knowing there'd be more to come.

"So how did you find me?" she asked.

Robert stood by the open windows trying to catch a breath of evening air. "Private detectives. They tracked you as far as Reno where you switched the plates on your car. Very clever, sis."

"Not clever enough, I guess." Although her little ruse had provided her with several weeks of soul-searching without interference from her family.

"They lost your trail after that. Mother was pretty frantic."

"I called her."

He glanced back over his shoulder. "Then we got word the sheriff in Grass Valley was asking about the switch."

Surprised, she turned to Walker, who was standing by the fireplace, his arms folded across his chest.

"I asked Eric to check the plates. I thought you might be in more trouble than you'd indicated."

He'd known before she told him that she wasn't from Nevada. She didn't know whether to be angry he'd been poking around trying to find out about her or not. It seemed only fair he'd want to check out a woman who'd showed up at his front door unannounced.

"Before we were able to follow up on that lead," Robert continued, "we got word you'd had a large amount of money transferred to a bank in Great Falls."

"Bail money," she said.

"Bail—" He choked. "Good God! Have you been arrested?"

"No, not me." She laughed. "The boys did a little joy riding in my car, is all. We're hoping the charges will be dropped."

Robert lifted a questioning brow. "Well, anyway, that's when I decided to get on a plane and come here. We were afraid something bad had happened to you. That maybe someone else was using your ID."

"Nothing bad's happened. I just needed to get away."

"She's an adult," Walker said, bristling. "She can go anywhere she wants."

"Sure. But it was a little sudden, right?"

Leaning back, Elizabeth brought the baby to her shoulder. "I didn't have the nerve to tell Mother—or Vernon—that I wanted to call off the wedding. So I ran away. Not very courageous of me, I'm afraid, and I'm sorry I ruined everyone's plans."

"I, for one, am damn glad she got out when she

could.'' Walker gave her brother a steely-eyed look, daring him to argue with him.

Moving away from the window, Robert parked himself on the arm of an overstuffed chair. ''Your leaving made me stop and think about Vernon, and do a little checking myself.''

''I know I upset Mother and I guess I did some damage to your political ambitions. I'm sorry—''

Her brother held up his hand to stop her. ''Vernon was furious when you ran off, but it wasn't like he'd lost the great love of his life.''

''I'd hurt his ego.''

''Possibly. But it was more than that, too.'' He leaned forward, resting his elbows on his thighs. ''What I learned is that Vernon is the black sheep of the Boston Spragues. I gather he did some dirty work there—making off with some of the family funds, leading some businesspeople to think he had more influence than he did.''

''You mean he wouldn't have been able to help you in the political arena?''

''You know, sis, that political stuff was Dad's idea. And Mom's. Not mine. I'm perfectly happy doing my lawyerly thing and going sailing on Sunday on the Bay, hanging out at the marina ogling the girls.'' He shrugged. ''Hard to beat that.''

''And all the time I thought—'' His revelation stunned her. Elizabeth had felt so guilty that she'd put her brother's ambitions at risk because of her own selfish weaknesses.

''After I got the scoop on Vernon, he and I had a

little chat," Robert continued. "He's pretty well out of the San Francisco picture now. Moved on to parts unknown. Which means it's safe for you to come home whenever you want, sis. Mom will be glad to see you and no hard feelings."

"Lately I've been thinking about going back to school but I'm not sure—"

Abruptly Walker unfolded his arms and his hands fell to his sides. "I forgot a meeting I scheduled for after supper." He shot Elizabeth a look so intense she couldn't translate its meaning. "I'll be back later. Don't leave until I come back."

"Leave? I'm not..."

He went striding from the room, leaving Elizabeth puzzled and frowning after him.

"What was that all about?" Robert asked.

She shook her head. "I have no idea." Walker wasn't normally moody but a cloud had certainly rained on him since her brother arrived.

As she heard Walker's truck drive off, she said, "Let's go sit on the porch. It's cooler there and Suzanne enjoys the fresh air."

Dark clouds piled up against the horizon to the north, lightning occasionally brightening in the distant sky. Sitting on the porch railing, Elizabeth took in the smell of the far-off rain, the closer scent of hay and horses, and heard the burst of adolescent laughter as the boys and Speed headed for the bunkhouse.

"When I first arrived here I thought how much Steve would have loved this place."

"Maybe for a few days but he wouldn't have stayed

long.'' Her brother settled on the glider, which squeaked as it accepted his weight. Stretching out his long legs, he crossed his ankles and cradled Susie-Q in his arms as though he held infants everyday. ''In fact, I never figured out how you two thought you'd actually get married someday.''

''How can you say that? We'd known each other forever. I fell in love with Steve when I was twelve. I never imagined marrying anyone else.''

''And every time you wanted to set the date, he went off somewhere. To college. A postcollege fling around Europe with his buddies.''

''A man needs his freedom before he settles down.''

''And then the oil drilling jaunt in South America that cost him his life.''

''*I* was the one who caused his death. He was coming back to—''

''Sis, if I ever fall in love with somebody, there's no way in hell I'll go off and leave her for a year unless they take me kicking and screaming.'' Shifting his weight, running an absent finger over the baby's cheek, he started the glider in motion. ''My best guess is, if things had gone as expected, Steve would have come up with some other trip he had to take, and you'd have been an old maid before you ever got to the altar.''

''That's not true!'' Elizabeth gasped. ''He loved me. He was coming back because—''

She turned away and gazed out at the darkening sky. Her pregnancy had forced Steve to act. He was too noble to leave her in the lurch, although he hadn't been thrilled by the thought of having a baby. He'd even planned, after the wedding, he'd return to the Amazon, finish the job there before they settled down.

Watching Suzanne grab playfully for Robert's nose, Elizabeth felt the truth knife through her, painfully slicing away the fantasy of Steve's love that had kept her going this past year. So many times she'd begged him to set a date. He'd kissed her, pleading for a chance for this one trip. One more adventure.

Tears burned in her eyes, blurring the lightning bolts in the distance.

He wouldn't have come back to marry her.

Why hadn't she seen that truth years ago? Because she'd been blinded by a childish love and had never allowed herself to grow up.

And maybe Steve was right to keep delaying their wedding plans. They'd been comfortable together but never once had she felt the same passion for Steve that she did for Walker, and she'd known him for a much shorter time.

"I'm sorry if I hurt your feelings, sis. I thought now that you've found someone else..."

She turned back to her brother. "You mean Walker?"

"The guy's nuts over you, way more than Steve ever was."

"No, you're wrong. He calls me a city slicker. He knows I'd never fit in on a ranch, not for the long haul."

"Boy, it didn't look like that to me tonight." He stood and crossed to the porch railing to stand beside her, transferring the baby back to her arms. "You whipped up a great meal for those hungry kids, enough food for a fair-size army, took care of Suzanne, played hostess to me. Looked to me like you were right at home here."

She laughed a humorless sound. "You should have seen all the meals I ruined until I got the hang of things."

"But you did learn. Seems to me that's all anyone could ask of you." He ran his palm over the top of Suzanne's head. "Would I be wrong if I guessed you've fallen in love with Walker?"

"No," she whispered. "You'd be right."

"Then I guess you won't be coming home with me."

"I can't stay here. I ran away because I wanted to find myself. I haven't—"

"I've watched you all evening, sister dearest. You're someone totally different than you were at home under Mother's thumb. You're stronger. More comfortable in your own skin, if that makes any sense. If you ask me, you ran away to exactly the right spot where you were meant to be. Maybe someday I'll be that lucky, too."

She looked up at him dumfounded. Had she really changed that much? Become the person she'd wanted to be without really noticing the difference?

"I felt so useless at home, doing nothing other than being a gofer at the foundation."

"They relied on you to evaluate dozens of different

charities every year and make recommendations about grant requests. The director valued your judgment.''

''I suppose he did, but—''

''And I suspect Mother was upset the most about you running away because that big shindig at the country club is coming up next month. You always did half the work but she got all the credit for putting on those affairs.''

''I never thought of it that way. I had to keep busy doing something.''

''Maybe if someone had bothered to thank you, you would have realized you're a heck of a sharp lady.''

Maybe so, she mused, but now...

The phone rang inside the house.

''I'd better get that. It might be Walker calling about something.'' She was still worried about his odd behavior when he'd left the house.

''Here,'' Robert said. ''Let me take the kid again while you get the phone.''

She grinned. ''You're an old softy, Uncle Robert.''

''Promise not to tell.''

Hurrying inside, Elizabeth took the call on the kitchen extension. ''Hello.''

''This is Mabel Cannery from social services. I apologize for calling so late but it's been one of those days.'' The woman exhaled a long, deep sigh. ''Is Walker there?''

''No, he said he had a meeting. This is Lizzie. Can I help you?''

''Yes, if you'd take a message, please.''

"Of course." Elizabeth found a pad of paper on the counter and a pencil. "Go ahead."

"Walker wanted me to let him know whenever one of his boys was officially available for adoption. This afternoon in Great Falls…"

Her hand poised over the pad of paper, Elizabeth listened with a combination of growing anger and excitement. Between Robert's revelations this evening and this phone call, she now knew exactly what she needed to do. She'd finally found herself.

Now all she needed was Walker's cooperation.

WALKER CURSED THE TIME it took to get to the Bar-X, argue with Harry Morgan and get back to the Double O. But he'd done what he set out to do. He'd made the deal that would have broken his dad's heart but he didn't know what else he could do.

Having Lizzie was a thousand times more important than owning a chunk of Montana grassland.

As he whipped into the long driveway to the ranch house, the first drop of rain landed on his windshield, turning dust to mud. And then a second drop hit. The storm that had been toying with the northern part of the state had finally dropped south.

Thank God! With luck, the storm would break the drought and his cows would have enough nutritious grass to graze on for the rest of the season.

He pulled his truck into its spot beside the barn. The bunkhouse was dark. So was the main house, except for a couple of lights on downstairs. Elizabeth must have left them on for him before she and her brother went to bed.

If she had sleep on her mind, she had another think coming. He wasn't going to wait till morning to share his news, the decision he'd made, and the hope he had for their future.

He hung his hat on the peg in the mudroom and walked into the kitchen. Lizzie was sitting at the table, dozing with her head resting on her elbow, a half-full coffee mug in front of her on the table. She'd loosened the pins from her hair, and it fell like a silver-blond waterfall past her face, hiding the delicate features he'd grown to love.

Startled, she looked up. "You're home!" She catapulted from the chair into his arms, and it was all he could do to catch her. "I was beginning to worry about you."

"I'm fine." More so now that he could wrap his arms around her and bury his face in the sweet scent of her shampoo. "Where's your brother?"

"He went to bed an hour ago. I wanted to wait up for you."

"Is something wrong?"

"No. Not at all. But I do have news."

He cringed, worried that she'd already made her plans to leave before he'd had a chance to tell her what he'd done, tell her about his dreams for them both.

Combing his fingers through her hair, he said, "I have news, too. Can I go first?"

Her smile crumpled, a frown marring her smooth forehead. "I suppose."

"I've sold my interest in the Double O to my neighbor, Harry Morgan."

"You've what?" she gasped.

"Well, the deal's not signed yet but I gave him my hand on it. I figured if you're going to go to school somewhere, I can go with you. If you pick somewhere like Colorado State at Fort Collins—"

"You've been checking the Internet for master's programs," she accused.

"Well, yeah, I thought I'd see where you might want to go to school—"

"You'd give up the Double O for me?"

"You're more important than anything else in the world."

"What about the boys?"

"I'll talk to Eric and Rory. Speed, too. We'll work out something."

She looked astonished by the prospect.

Walker wasn't. When a man found a woman he wanted to spend the rest of his life with, a ranch meant less than nothing. *She* meant everything and always would.

"I can get a job anywhere, and if it's ranching country, I can buy—"

"What if I don't want to go anywhere but right here?"

"Huh?" This wasn't the reaction he'd anticipated. He half expected her to tell him to get lost. He'd hoped she'd think it was a great idea. But stay here? He'd already sold his share—

"Mabel Cannery called earlier."

With difficulty, he forced his brain to shift topics. "Something wrong with the boys?"

"Yes and no. The police picked up Scotty's mother and her boyfriend on new possession charges plus jumping bail. Apparently Mabel talked with the woman, and she agreed to relinquish all parental rights to Scotty."

"You're kidding! That means I can adopt—"

"Yes, you can adopt Scotty." She grinned up at him like a cat who'd enjoyed every morsel of a canary she'd caught.

"You knew that's what I wanted, didn't you?"

"I had that feeling. Oliver Oakes did the same for you."

"Yeah." The memories of the day he and Oliver had stood in front of a judge washed over him. Knowing, *finally,* that he had a place to call home. Forever. The Double O—which he'd just sold to Harry Morgan. "Damn!" he muttered. "I can't—"

"There's more."

He rolled his eyes. He'd already messed up his chance to adopt Scotty by planning to move out of state. What more could there be?

"Scotty's mother has also relinquished his sister. Her name's Nancy, she's two and a half and adorable, according to Mabel. She'll have to go into foster care unless—" she palmed his cheek, which was rough with evening whiskers "—unless we adopt her, too."

"I can't take care of a baby. There's no way—" His brain ground to a halt, the mental brakes all but smoking he stopped so quickly, and circled back over what she'd said. "We?"

"See, I know you don't have time to run the ranch *and* take care of a toddler plus the boys, but there's nothing that says I can't do that."

"You?"

"If I stayed on at the Double O. As a house-keeper—" Standing on tiptoe, she brushed a kiss to his lips. "Or your wife, if you'd be interested."

His knees went weak. He'd never expected... He'd figured he'd have to leave... He couldn't quite grasp... "I gave my word to Harry."

"So take it back. I'm sure he'll understand."

"What about your master's degree? Your education?"

"I suspect being your wife will be education enough, and I'll have plenty of chances to use every bit of psychology I know."

"Your trust fund. I don't want people to think I married you for your—"

"It will be *our* money. A rancher can always use something tucked away for a rainy day, can't he? And maybe Harry Morgan will let us buy *his* land someday."

Walker swallowed so hard he nearly choked. "You want to marry me?"

"That's what I have in mind, unless you're prepared to put up with burned meals concocted by a woman scorned."

"No. I wouldn't want that." My God, what was he

supposed to do now? "Lizzie, I, huh, yes, I like your plan better than mine."

"Good. But there is one little detail…well, two, really. Do you love me?"

"Absolutely." He leaned his head back and howled, but not nearly as loud as the storm raging outside had become. The earth at last finding renewal. Clear, cool refreshment flowing down the mountains and through the grassland.

He was coming alive, too, after a long drought. "I swear, I'll love you till I die and beyond." He dropped his head to kiss her but she held him off.

"The second item of business is that I want to set the wedding date right now. I want it soon, and there'll be no backing out, right?"

"Would tomorrow be soon enough?"

She laughed, a wonderfully lighthearted sound. "Tomorrow would be fine, but maybe we ought to give the preacher and our respective families a little more time to get used to the idea. Say a week from Saturday?"

"Perfect." He claimed her mouth then. His to taste, to possess and to love for as long as he wanted, and he was going to savor every moment.

Which he did until a wayward thought entered his head. He backed off. "You're not marrying me just because you feel sorry for Scotty and his sister, are you?"

"Scotty's cute," she said with a sappy grin, "but you're the man I love. Forever and a day, Walker Oakes. Forever and a day."

Epilogue

Overnight the landscape changed and within a week drought-dry grass had turned green, shooting up to knee-high. The air was ripe with the scent of the new growth and Grass Valley was alive with excitement over the upcoming wedding.

In his way, Harry Morgan seemed the most delighted the deal to buy the Double O had been called off. "If I owned ol' Oliver's ranch, what would I have left to grouse about," the elderly gentleman said before winking at Elizabeth. "'Course, if a pretty little filly like you was to make an offer on my place..."

By Saturday, Elizabeth could barely contain her happiness. Even her mother seemed resigned to the far more modest wedding than the one she had originally planned for her daughter.

Standing in the minister's office at the Grass Valley church, Dorthea Tilden fussed with the wisp of a veil Elizabeth had selected off the rack in a bridal store in Great Falls only four days ago.

"I really don't see why you couldn't have worn the

gown from Gloriana's,'' her mother said. "You were such a striking bride in it.''

"Mother, the train was longer than the entire center aisle in this church. This dress suits me much better.'' She'd selected a pale green, knee-length sheath in silk, a far cry from the lace and pearl-studded gown that she'd tucked away in the trunk of her car six weeks ago. That one would find its way back to Gloriana's, where it could be put to better use.

"I know, dear. And you do look lovely.''

"That's because I'm happy. Wish me well, won't you?''

"Oh, I do, dear. And you're going to need all the luck you can get, starting off your marriage with *six* children in the house and no servants.''

"We'll manage, Mother. In fact, I'm thinking I could put grandmother's trust fund to good use by hiring extra help.'' Because, if Elizabeth had her way, there'd be more children later—as soon as Susie-Q was safely out of diapers. There were lots of bedrooms to fill at the Double O. A perfect home for the loving family she'd always wanted.

She glanced down at her fingernails, not long but polished in a soft shade of rose because Walker had asked her to. Soon enough the polish would chip but for their all-too brief honeymoon she was more than willing to indulge his fantasies. And hers.

Elizabeth's sister Victoria, who was her matron of honor, stuck her head in the door. She had a tight grip on Scotty's little sister Nancy's hand, who had an equally firm grip on her basket of rose petals. The child's red hair was even brighter than Scotty's, and both youngsters would soon be official members of the growing Oakes family. Fortunately for the boys, Robert had made a few phone calls, using his influence and connections to get the charges against them dropped.

With luck, he'd also be able to expedite Elizabeth and Walker adopting the other boys, too.

"They're ready for you, Mother," Victoria said. "Walker and his brothers have started to pace like caged animals. Very handsome animals, I might add." She shared a private look with Elizabeth. "I'd say you have an eager groom on your hands."

"No more eager than I am."

"Oh, posh!" Dorthea blushed. "You girls shouldn't talk like that."

Since her family had arrived in Montana two nights ago, out of deference Elizabeth had stayed with them at a motel in Shelby. She'd desperately missed Walker and could hardly wait to see him again, be in his arms again.

"Is your father out there?" her mother asked.

"Pacing with the men."

"Very well." Dorthea Tilden drew back her shoulders and stretched to her full five-foot-three height. At fifty, her skin was unwrinkled, her complexion still lovely and not a single strand of gray showed in her perfectly styled blond hair. A formidable woman but not one suited to ranch life.

Elizabeth felt she'd been created for that role.

Minutes later she stood in the vestibule, her hand wrapped around her father's arm and caught her first sight of Walker. Standing in front of the altar straight and tall, dressed in a Western-cut beige jacket with darker pants, he simply took her breath away.

A feeling of rightness settled over her. She smiled at him and took her first step toward the rest of her life with the man she loved.

This time, there'd be no running away.

WALKER HAD BEEN SURE he'd either throw up or faint until she showed up at the entrance to the church sanctuary, her hair curled and piled high on her head with artful wisps teasing the tempting column of her neck. Then she smiled at him from the opposite end of the church aisle. In that instant, his entire world turned right side up for the first time in years.

She loved him. Even across the length of the church, he could see it in her eyes. For reasons he couldn't fathom, she found him worthy of that love as no other woman had. He vowed he'd never give her any reason to doubt her gift to him. In return, she'd have every ounce of his love to hold in her heart for as long as she wanted it.

In unison, both of his brothers nudged him forward.

"Go get her, Sharpy," Eric said. "You're a lucky son of gun."

"You white eyes have all the luck," Rory commented.

He glanced at his two "best men" and his chest swelled with pride and another kind of love.

"You two guys will get your turn. I'm sure of it." With that, he stepped forward to claim the woman he'd love for the rest of his life.

And beyond.

* * * * *

Watch for Rory's and Eric's stories,
coming from Harlequin American Romance
in 2003.

Say "I do" with

AMERICAN *Romance*®

and
Kara Lennox

**First you tempt him. Then you tame him...
all the way to the altar.**

PLAIN JANE'S PLAN
October 2002

Plain Jane Allison Crane knew her chance had finally
come to catch the eye of her lifelong crush, Jeff Hardison.
With a little help from a friend—and one great big
makeover—could Allison finally win her heart's desire?

Don't miss the other titles in this series:

VIXEN IN DISGUISE
August 2002

SASSY CINDERELLA
December 2002

HARLEQUIN®
Makes any time special®

HARHTMAH2

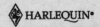

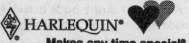